AB
821
H31397

£15.99

D0493408

WAR POEMS

Christopher Martin

Ploughing the waste, we turn up from the clay
The bones of warriors in some old affray
Fallen: but, what they fought for in their day,
Or who the victors were, now none can say.

WILFRID GIBSON: *THE VICTORS*

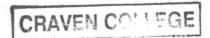
CRAVEN COLLEGE

Collins

Published by HarperCollinsPublishers Limited
77-85 Fulham Palace Rd
Hammersmith
London W6 8JB

www.CollinsEducation.com
On-line support for schools and colleges

©HarperCollinsPublishers 2004

10 9 8 7
ISBN-13 978 0 00 717746 2
ISBN-10 0 00 717746 1

Christopher Martin asserts the moral right to be identified as the
author of this work.

All rights reserved. No part of this publication may be reproduced,
stored in a retrieval system, or transmitted in any form or by any
means, electronic, mechanical, photocopying, recording or otherwise,
without the prior permission of the Publisher or a licence permitting
restricted copying in the United Kingdom issued by the Copyright
Licensing Agency Ltd, 90 Tottenham Court Rd, London W1P 9HE.

British Library Cataloguing in Publication Data.

A catalogue record for this publication is available from the
British Library.

DESIGN BY: bluepigdesign
ILLUSTRATION: *Gassed* by John Singer Sargent, ©Imperial War Museum
COVER DESIGN BY: ABA Design
COMMISSIONING EDITOR: Isabelle Zahar
EDITED BY: Mark Dudgeon

CONTENTS

PREFACE TO SECOND EDITION

Grim new chapters in the history of war – in Iraq, in the Balkans and in Africa – have been written since this book first appeared in 1990. During the same time, interest in the great World Wars of the early twentieth century has grown more intense, with excellent new TV series, films, novels, biographies, histories and internet sites. The Somme and Passchendaele, the Holocaust and Hiroshima still haunt our imaginations.

The extraordinary poetry of the World Wars also continues to fascinate us. Perhaps, since 1990, we have grown less angry about mud, blood and futility, and more thoughtful about the courage, endurance and suffering of the men and women who experienced the war years. And there have been some poetic surprises and discoveries: fresh editions of Ivor Gurney's poetry that at last show his full genius; a lost manuscript version of Wilfred Owen's *Anthem for Doomed Youth*, and, amazingly, several new war poems by Siegfried Sassoon.

This second edition reflects some of these developments and changes in thinking about war and war poetry. A core of poems for study that has proved popular in GCSE work has been retained. New poems – chosen for their freshness and vividness – have been added. Study notes and work ideas, especially on 'set' poems, have been up-dated in line with National Curriculum requirements. Splendid colour pictures – many little known – add enormously to the impact of the book. Finally, the 'Further reading' list has become a resources guide that includes internet sites as well as books and audio-visual material.

Christopher Martin 2004

INTRODUCTION

War: the glory and the horror

ON THE IDLE HILL

On the idle hill of summer,
    Sleepy with the flow of streams,
Far I hear the steady drummer
    Drumming like a noise in dreams.

Far and near and low and louder
    On the roads of earth go by,
Dear to friends and food for powder,
    Soldiers marching, all to die.

East and west on fields forgotten
    Bleach the bones of comrades slain,
Lovely lads and dead and rotten;
    None that go return again.

Far the calling bugles hollo,
    High the screaming fife replies,
Gay the files of scarlet follow:
    Woman bore me, I will rise.

A.E. HOUSMAN
from A Shropshire lad: 35

A.E. Housman was not thinking of a particular war when he wrote this poem in 1896. It is a beautifully balanced general comment on the glamour and the horror of battle. Peace is dull: 'idle' and 'sleepy'. The summons to war has a magnetic attraction with the haunting military music and the hypnotic drum which no young man can resist. Yet the excitement and splendour lead only to death and destruction. Everyone will die, no matter how they are loved, and battlefields and victories are quickly forgotten. Housman sums up what most of us feel about war: it is exciting and fascinating to study but it is also horrible, pointless and mad.

Late Victorian poetry is a good source for contrasting views of war as glory or horror. Some poets were much less subtle than Housman. W.E. Henley praised violence in his fearsome poem The song of the sword (1892). In Epilogue (1901), he was impatient with the long peace that Britain had enjoyed since the Crimean War of the 1850s. Peace was 'a golden fog', 'a dream of money and love and sport' that made the nation 'fattening, mellowing, dozing, rotting down'. The Boer War, that began in 1899, would bring Britain back to life:

With a million-throated shouting, swoops and storms
War, the Red Angel, the Awakener,
The Shaker of Souls and thrones...

By contrast, Berman Neuman, writing in 1905, had lost friends in the confused battles in South Africa, and had read of thousands of soldiers dying from disease, and of the cruelties of the so-called 'concentration camps' that defeated the Boers. He ends a sequence of Boer War poems with a vision of the temple of the War-God, much influenced by the fantasy paintings of the time. The huge temple looks glamorous on the outside but, when you enter, you find the truth about war.

THE SHRINE OF THE WAR-GOD

Splendid, upon a bare and blasted plain,
    It rose before me in the sunset light,
Vast, many-towered, like some majestic fane[1]
    With one great cross of gold to crown its height.

And then I looked within; a poison-breath,
    Sickened me, and I saw the temple's Lord
Stalk up and down his festering house of death,
    A naked savage with a dripping sword.

BERMAN NEUMAN

[1] fane: temple

As an introduction to the poems that follow, look at the paired pictures on the following pages that show contrasting aspects of war.

The first two pictures are about the battle of Waterloo, fought in June 1815, when British and German troops defeated Napoleon's French army. One is by the Victorian artist, Elizabeth Butler, who specialized in battle scenes. The other is a watercolour of battle-wounded, painted just after the fighting by an army surgeon, Charles Bell.

The Scots' Grey charge at Waterloo: Elizabeth Butler

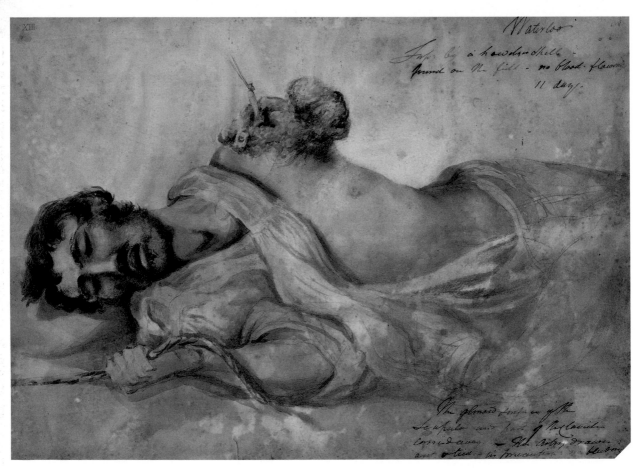

Wounded soldier after Waterloo painted by an army surgeon, Charles Bell

French poster of 1916

The outbreak of war in August 1914 was greeted with enthusiasm by Europe's young men, who saw it as a great adventure and test of manhood. This French poster, with its slogan 'On les aura!' ('We're going to get them!'), catches the mood. Yet this war killed more than eight and a half million men. Here is just one of them: a German killed at the Somme in November 1916.

German corpse, Beaumont-Hamel, the Somme, November 1916

British recruiting poster

Grieving German woman: Käthe Kollwitz

These contrasting images of women in war date from 1914–18. The first is a recruiting poster, aimed at persuading men to volunteer for the British Army; the second, a drawing by the German artist, Käthe Kollwitz, shows the effect on a woman of news of her husband's death at the Front. 'Opfer' means 'victim' or 'sacrifice'.

🐚 DISCUSSION

What do the paired pictures tell us about war, and people's attitudes to it? What are your own feelings about the contrasts that you see there? Which pair do you find most forceful and dramatic? Try to explain why.

✏️ WRITING

Choose one of the pairs of pictures. Write briefly and imaginatively about each image, identifying yourself, perhaps, with the people that you see there. Your writing should make clear what the pictures tell us about the glamour and horror of war.

📖 COMPARING POEMS

To conclude this Introduction, read the two poems on the next page written by civilians as the First World War began in August 1914. If these were days of public excitement and patriotic hysteria, there were also anxiety and depression as people began to understand the death and destruction involved in a massive European war that used twentieth-century weapons.

Soldiers, despised in the nineteenth century, now became heroes. Military parades drew huge crowds. A Liverpool reporter watched local volunteers march through the city: 'There was no vain glory about this display – there was the tramp, tramp of smart, well set up young gentlemen, shoulders thrown back and faces stern and resolute'. Captivating military music added to the mood. A young volunteer, George Coppard, remembered how 'News placards screamed out at every street corner and military bands blared out their martial music'.

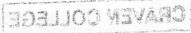
CRAVEN COLLEGE

FOR TWO VOICES

'O mother, mother, isn't it fun,
    The soldiers marching past in the sun!'
'Child, child, what are you saying?
    Come to church. We should be praying.'

'Look, mother, at their bright spears!'
    'The leaves are falling like women's tears.'
'You are not looking at what I see.'
    'Nay, but I look at what must be.'

'Hark to the pipers! See the flags flying!'
    'I hear the sound of a girl crying.'
'How many hundreds before they are done?'
    'How many mothers wanting a son?'

'Here rides the general, pacing slow!'
    'Well he may, if he knows what I know.'
'O this war, what a glorious game!'
    'Sin and shame, sin and shame.'

MAURICE HEWLETT, August 1914

CLOSE STUDY

1 The poem is narrated by two people, a mother and her young son. By studying the speech punctuation, work out who is saying which lines. Then, with a partner, read the poem aloud.

2 What various features of the parade attract the son? Make a list of them.

3 What does the mother think of as she watches the marching soldiers? List her worries.

4 What is the poet's final conclusion about war in this well-balanced discussion?

from: THE ILLUSION OF WAR

War
I abhor,[1]
And yet how sweet
The sound along the marching street
Of drum and fife, and I forget
Wet eyes of widows, and forget
Broken old mothers, and the whole
Dark butchery without a soul.

Without a soul – save this bright drink
Of heady music, sweet as hell;
And even my peace-abiding feet
Go marching with the marching street,
For yonder yonder goes the fife,
And what care I for human life!…

Art, thou hast many infamies,[2]
But not an infamy like this.
O snap the fife and still the drum,
And show the monster as she is.

RICHARD LE GALLIENNE

[1] **abhor:** *hate*
[2] **infamies:** *wicked faults*

CLOSE STUDY

1 Despite his anti-war attitudes, the poet finds himself carried away by military music. Which words and phrases express its magic?

2 What does the excitement of the music make him forget?

3 Which two lines describe the ugly reality of war?

DISCUSSION

With a partner, compare the two poems, looking at

- their language and **style**
- their messages about war

Which poem do you find more impressive?

CRAVEN COLLEGE

PART 1

THE NAPOLEONIC ERA TO THE BOER WAR

War poetry brings history to life by telling us the private thoughts of men and women who have experienced conflict between nations. There were few soldier poets before the end of the nineteenth century. Most men who fought the endless battles were illiterate, and their thoughts are lost to us. There are a few glimpses. Joseph Hall was writing in Shakespeare's time when there was fighting in Flanders, but his soldier, who longs to escape from battle to return home to his ploughing, sounds like someone from Flanders, 1917.

> Oh war! To them that never tried thee, sweet!
> When his dead mate falls grovelling at his feet,
> And angry bullets whistle at his ear,
> And his dim eyes see naught but death and drere-
> Oh happy ploughman …

from *Satire 6*: 1597

The many women poets of the eighteenth century also considered war. Anne Finch, Countess of Winchelsea, in *All is vanity* (1713) was sad that the glamour of military uniforms lured young men to death in battle.

> Trail all your pikes, dispirit every drum,
> March in a slow procession from afar,
> Be silent, ye dejected Men of war!
> Be still the hautboys,[1] and the flute be dumb!
> Display no more, in vain, the lofty banner;
> For see! where on the bier before ye lies
> The pale, the fall'n, the untimely sacrifice
> To your mistaken shrine, to your false idol, Honour.
>
> *ANNE FINCH*
>
> [1] **hautboys:** *oboes*

The chaos of a seventeenth-century battle: there were no soldier poets to describe what the fighting was like

UNIT 1 //
War against Napoleon

The long series of struggles (1792–1815) between revolutionary France and rival European powers made up the first modern 'total war' and created the first extensive writing of war poetry. Not only were there huge armies in the field and great fleets at sea but also journalists were able to stir up civilian populations to patriotic fury. However, there was also strong anti-war writing.

from: FEARS IN SOLITUDE

Secure from actual warfare, we have loved
To swell the war-whoop, passionate for war! ...
        ... Boys and girls,
And women, that would groan to see a child
Pull off an insect's leg, all read of war,
The best amusement for our morning meal! ...
As if the soldier died without a wound, ...
As though he had no wife to pine for him...

S.T. COLERIDGE

Napoleon, a French Revolutionary General, became the dictator (1799) and then Emperor (1804) of France. His ambitions to dominate Europe were restrained by defeats in Russia (1812) and Spain (1814), which forced him to abdicate. He escaped exile on the Isle of Elba to form a new French army, that was finally crushed at Waterloo (1815).

W.M. Thackeray, the Victorian novelist, was fascinated by the Napoleonic era. He wrote this poem about Napoleon and the futility of his military conquests.

NAPOLEON

He captured many thousand guns;
He wrote 'The Great' before his name;
And dying, only left his sons
The recollection of his shame.
Though more than half the world was his,
He died without a rood[1] his own;
And borrowed from his enemies
Six foot of ground to lie upon.
He fought a thousand glorious wars,
And more than half the world was his,
And somewhere, now, in yonder stars,
Can tell, mayhap,[2] what greatness is.

W.M. THACKERAY

[1] **rood:** *quarter acre*
[2] **mayhap:** *perhaps*

What various points is Thackeray making about the 'glory' of Napoleon's career?

📖 COMPARING POEMS

Compare this poem with Southey's *The Battle of Blenheim* (p.13).

Think about

- the way the poems are narrated
- the pictures they give of military conquest
- the points they make about 'greatness'.

Which is more forceful and memorable?

John Scott was a Quaker and therefore opposed to all violence. He wrote *The Drum* in 1782 but it remained very popular and was reprinted many times during the Napoleonic era. For centuries what Shakespeare called the 'spirit-stirring drum' had been used by recruiting officers to attract men into the Army.

THE DRUM

I hate that drum's discordant sound,
Parading round, and round, and round:
To thoughtless youth it pleasure yields,
And lures from cities and from fields,
To sell their liberty for charms
Of tawdry[1] lace, and glittering arms;
And when Ambition's voice commands,
To march, and fight, and fall, in foreign lands.

I hate that drum's discordant sound,
Parading round, and round, and round:
To me it talks of ravaged plains,
And burning towns, and ruined swains[2],
And mangled limbs, and dying groans,
And widows' tears, and orphans' moans;
And all that Misery's hand bestows,
To fill the catalogue of human woes.

JOHN SCOTT

[1] **tawdry:** *cheap and showy (lace was used in officers' uniforms)*
[2] **swains:** *young men*

CRAVEN COLLEGE

CLOSE STUDY

1 What pictures of the attractive side of army life does the drum produce in young men's minds?

2 What is the key word in the first stanza?

3 What grim details of war does the drum produce in Scott's mind?

4 What is the key word in the second stanza?

5 How does the **rhythm** of the poem imitate the sound of the drum?

6 The poem has been admired for the perfect balance of its stanzas. Look closely at the ideas of each stanza and explain how one contrasts with the other.

7 The last line in each stanza is longer than the others. What effect does this have?

WRITING

1 Write about the poem, outlining its main ideas and saying what you find interesting in the way it is written. Consider:

- the poem's ideas
- the use of language
- the rhythm and use of rhyme
- the structure of the poem.

2 Study the cartoon, *John Bull's progress* by James Gillray. It has roughly the same theme as *The Drum*. Write descriptively or imaginatively about what is happening in each picture. Say how the cartoon is like the poem and which you find more impressive.

John Bull's progress: James Gillray, 1793

Robert Southey wrote *The Battle of Blenheim* for *The Morning Post* in 1798, as part of its opposition to war with revolutionary France.

To support this theme, he looks back to the Wars of the Spanish Succession at the beginning of the century, especially to the great Anglo-Austrian victory at Blenheim in Austria (13 August 1704). The Allied commanders, the Duke of Marlborough and Prince Eugene of Savoy, surprised Louis XIV's army near Vienna after a dramatic march across Europe. Fifty thousand men died. French power was smashed.

Southey believes that war is a futile way to settle disputes, and that military success and glory are soon forgotten. He illustrates these ideas by the story of old Kaspar, an Austrian peasant who lives on the former battlefield.

THE BATTLE OF BLENHEIM

I
It was a summer evening,
    Old Kaspar's work was done,
And he before his cottage door
    Was sitting in the sun,
And by him sported on the green
His little grandchild Wilhelmine.

II
She saw her brother Peterkin
    Roll something large and round,
Which he beside the rivulet
    In playing there had found;
He came to ask what he had found,
That was so large, and smooth, and round.

III
Old Kaspar took it from the boy,
    Who stood expectant by;
And then the old man shook his head,
    And, with a natural sigh,
    'Tis some poor fellow's skull,' said he,
'Who fell in the great victory.

IV
'I find them in the garden,
    For there's many here about;
And often when I go to plough,
    The ploughshare turns them out!
For many thousand men,' said he,
'Were slain in that great victory.'

V
'Now tell us what 'twas all about,'
    Young Peterkin, he cries;
And little Wilhelmine looks up
    With wonder-waiting eyes;
'Now tell us all about the war,
And what they fought each other for.'

VI
'It was the English,' Kaspar cried,
    'Who put the French to rout;
But what they fought each other for,
    I could not well make out;
But everybody said,' quoth he,
'That 'twas a famous victory.

VII
'My father lived at Blenheim then,
    Yon little stream hard by;
They burnt his dwelling to the ground,
    And he was forced to fly;
So with his wife and child he fled,
Nor had he where to rest his head.

VIII
'With fire and sword the country round
    Was wasted far and wide,
And many a childing mother then,
    And new-born baby died;
But things like that, you know, must be
At every famous victory.

IX
'They say it was a shocking sight
    After the field was won;
For many thousand bodies here
    Lay rotting in the sun;
But things like that, you know, must be
After a famous victory.

X
'Great praise the Duke of Marlbro' won,
    And our good Prince Eugene.'[1]
'Why 'twas a very wicked thing!'
    Said little Wilhelmine.
'Nay … nay …my little girl,' quoth he,
'It was a famous victory.

XI
'And everybody praised the Duke
    Who this great fight did win.'
'But what good came of it at last?'
    Quoth little Peterkin.
'Why that I cannot tell,' said he
'But 'twas a famous victory.'

ROBERT SOUTHEY

[1] **Marlbro / Eugene:** *the Allied commanders*

1. Describe the setting in stanza 1.

2. What does Peterkin find that starts the discussion of the Battle?

3. Why is Kaspar used to such finds?

4. What terrible details of the Battle does he recall?

5. What does he fail to understand?

6. Like Wordsworth, Southey thought that children have insights into life that older people do not have. How does Southey use the children here to expose the pointlessness of war?

7. What has happened to the phrases 'great victory' and 'famous victory' by the end of the poem?

8. What does it tell us about the horror and waste of war?

9. The poem is a **ballad**. This is a **narrative** (story) which has a simple rhyming **style**, concise action and **dialogue** (use of conversation).

   Why is the simple style:
   - suitable?
   - very effective for conveying Southey's ideas about war?

1. Write your own conversation (it need not be a poem, but could be a play script or story extract) between modern children and their grandfather, who is telling them about a war in recent history that he remembers. Perhaps their conversation is prompted by wartime relics: *medals, a photo, an old shell case*.

   Base the argument closely on *Blenheim* so that you can put across the same message about war.

2. Study this painting, *Two skeletons fighting over a red herring*, by James Ensor. It is like *The Battle of Blenheim* in its fierce attack on war. Consider how exactly it is like and unlike the poem. Write your own ballad poem or very short story based on the painting.

Two soldier skeletons fighting over a red herring: James Ensor

THE BATTLE OF WATERLOO

The battle of 18 June 1815 marked the final defeat of Emperor Napoleon's ambitions to make the French the masters of Europe. British and German armies, led by Wellington and Blucher, won the day at Waterloo, a Belgian village near Brussels.

Lord Byron, writing just after the great battle brilliantly recreated the fear and excitement of Brussels on the eve of the fighting.

> ... the beat of the alarming drum
>   Roused up the soldier ere the morning star;
>   While thronged the citizens with terror dumb,
> Or whispering, with white lips – 'The foe! they come! they come!'
>
> *LORD BYRON,*
> Childe Harold, Canto 3, 1816

Later in the nineteenth century, the German poet, Rainer Maria Rilke, looked back on the same night. He imagined a young officer saying goodbye to his wife before he went into battle. (The German Brunswicker – Prussian – troops fought under Wellington's command. They wore a black plumed hat, a *shako*, grimly decorated with a skull-and-crossbones badge as in the picture below.)

BEFORE WATERLOO, THE LAST NIGHT

And night and muffled creakings and the wheels
of the artillery-wagons circling with the clock,
Blucher's[1] Prussian army passing the estate. ...
The man plays the harpsichord, and lifts his eyes,
playing each air by ear to look at her –
he might be looking in a mirror for himself,
a mirror filled with his young face, the sorrow
his music made seductive and beautiful.
Suddenly everything is over. Instead,
Wearily by an open window, she stands
and clasps the helpless thumping of her heart.
No sound. Outside, a fresh morning wind has risen,
and strangely foreign on the mirror-table,
leans his black shako with its white deathshead.

RAINER MARIA RILKE
(*translated by Robert Lowell*)

[1] **Blucher:** *commander of Prussian (German) army*

● CLOSE STUDY

1   What is the scene? What is the **mood**? What is happening outside?

2   Why are the couple speechless? What do you imagine are their thoughts?

3   Why is the man playing the harpsichord?

4   How do the silence and the morning wind change the mood at the end?

5   What do man and woman think of as they look at the black shako in the last line?

✐ WRITING

Write the story of the poem using this painting to help you with details. First describe the room and what is in it. Mention the sounds that create the atmosphere. Give the thoughts of the man and the woman's thoughts and fears. End with the couple looking in horror at the death's head badge on the shako just before the man leaves for battle.

Parting before Waterloo: *The black Brunswicker:* J.E. Millais

UNIT 2 //
The Crimean War 1854-6

Britain and France feared Russia's ambition to spread its power southwards as the Turkish Empire collapsed. War broke out in 1854. In September, the Allies landed in the Crimea, in southern Russia, and besieged Sebastopol. In October the Russians attacked the British base at Balaclava.

During this battle, the disastrous Charge of the Light Brigade took place. The British cavalry commander mistook his orders to retake some guns held by the Russians. Instead he told his men to charge the main Russian position, which was at the head of a valley bristling with artillery. The 600 horsemen gallantly obeyed but two thirds of the force were killed or wounded. The Charge is the best known example of the heroism and stupidity of war.

W.H. Russell, a correspondent for *The Times*, became famous for his reports from the Crimea. This is how he described the Charge.

The Times, 14 November 1854

At ten minutes past eleven our Light Cavalry Brigade advanced… They swept proudly past, glittering in the morning sun in all the pride and splendour of war… At the distance of 1,200 yards the whole line of the enemy belched forth, from thirty iron mouths, a flood of smoke and flame. The flight was marked by instant gaps in our ranks, by dead men and horses, by steeds flying wounded or riderless across the plain. In diminished ranks, with a halo of steel above their heads, and with a cheer which was many a noble fellow's death cry, they flew into the smoke of the batteries; but ere they were lost from view the plain was strewn with their bodies. Through the clouds of smoke we could see their sabres flashing as they rode between the guns, cutting down the gunners as they stood. We saw them riding through, returning, after breaking through a column of Russians and scattering them like chaff, when the flank fire of the batteries on the hill swept them down. Wounded men and dismounted troopers flying towards us told the sad tale… at thirty-five minutes past eleven not a British soldier, except the dead and the dying, was left in front of the Muscovite guns.

'*All that was left of them*': dead cavalryman and horse from the Charge, drawn in 1855 by Henry Crealock

Alfred Tennyson was **Poet Laureate**. He read Russell's report. His son described how he wrote his poem 'in a few minutes after reading *The Times* in which occurred the phrase "someone had blundered" and this was the origin of the metre of his poem'. Not everyone liked it: a critic saw it as 'a real gallop in verse and only good as such', while Tennyson himself noted that it was 'not a poem on which I pique myself', but it has remained popular and famous as a study of the glamour and futility of war.

THE CHARGE OF THE LIGHT BRIGADE

I

Half a league, half a league,
  Half a league onward,
All in the valley of Death
  Rode the six hundred.
'Forward, the Light Brigade!
Charge for the guns!' he said:
Into the valley of Death
  Rode the six hundred.

II

'Forward, the Light Brigade!'
Was there a man dismayed?
Not though the soldier knew
  Some one had blundered:
Their's[1] not to make reply,
Their's not to reason why,
Their's but to do and die:
Into the valley of Death
  Rode the six hundred.

III

Cannon to right of them,
Cannon to left of them,
Cannon in front of them
  Volleyed and thundered;
Stormed at with shot and shell,
Boldly they rode and well,
Into the jaws of Death,
Into the mouth of Hell
  Rode the six hundred.

IV

Flashed all their sabres[2] bare,
Flashed as they turned in air
Sabring the gunners there,
Charging an army, while
  All the world wondered:
Plunged in the battery-smoke
Right through the line they broke;
Cossack and Russian
Reeled from the sabre-stroke
  Shattered and sundered.
Then they rode back, but not
  Not the six hundred.

V

Cannon to right of them,
Cannon to left of them,
Cannon behind them
  Volleyed and thundered;
Stormed at with shot and shell,
While horse and hero fell,
They that had fought so well
Came through the jaws of Death,
Back from the mouth of Hell,
All that was left of them,
  Left of six hundred.

VI

When can their glory fade?
O the wild charge they made!
  All the world wondered.
Honour the charge they made!
Honour the Light Brigade,
  Noble six hundred!

ALFRED TENNYSON

[1] **Their's:** *Tennyson's old fashioned punctuation*
[2] **sabres:** *long swords with curved blades*

CLOSE STUDY

Stanzas 1-3

These describe the charge towards the Russian guns, 'into the jaws of death'.

1   What does Tennyson mean by:
    Their's not to reason why,
    Their's but to do and die:?

2   Which line tells you a mistake had been made?

3   What creates the beating **rhythm** of the poem and what does it imitate?

4   Look at the four lines starting 'cannon to right of them'. The short syllables are **onomatopoeic** (their sound imitates what they are describing). What sounds are those lines imitating?

Stanzas 4-5

The brigade reaches the Russian guns and attacks the gun crews with sabres. Tennyson catches the glamour without the horror of the bloodshed.

5   Which idea did Tennyson borrow from Russell here?

6   Why repeat 'not' at the end of stanza 4?

Stanza 6

Tennyson stands back to offer general comment on an epic moment of war. A French general who watched the Charge said, 'It is magnificent, but it is not war: it is folly'.

7   How does Tennyson's comment disagree with this?

8   Where does Tennyson show his pity for the soldiers?

9   What, finally, do you think that he felt about the Charge?

1   Write your own newspaper front page story about the Charge. Your aim should be to inform readers and describe the events in an engaging way. Take most ideas and details from the poem, but also use Russell. Add an editorial responding to the event, commenting generally on the grandeur, and the waste, of the attack.

2   Look at these contrasting pictures. Then write an account of the Charge in the form of two descriptive sketches. You might choose to write them as recollections by two of the survivors. Use ideas and details from the report, the poem, and the two pictures.

The Charge of the Light Brigade: Caton Woodville

After the Charge: Elizabeth Butler

UNIT 3 //

The American Civil War 1861-5

The ferocious war between the Northern Union states and the Southern Confederacy began in June 1861. The North, led by President Lincoln, wished to end slavery; the South resisted fiercely and decided to leave the Union. The Northern victory in the bloody battle of Gettysburg, in July 1863, was the turning-point that led to the final defeat of the South in 1865.

Walt Whitman's first war poems reflected the general excitement about the conflict in the northern American cities. His attitudes were transformed, however, by the wounding of his younger brother in battle, and his work as a 'wound-dresser' in a Washington hospital.

In the poem on the next page, Whitman writes imaginatively about the effects of war on a farming family from Ohio (Ohio was on the Northern side). A letter from the front tells them bad news about their son, Pete

> Spent a good part of the day in a large brick mansion used as a hospital since the battle – seems to have received all the worst cases. Outdoors, at the foot of a tree, I notice a heap of amputated feet, legs, arms, hands etc., a full load for a one horse cart. Several dead bodies lie near, each covered with its brown woollen blanket. In the dooryard are fresh graves, mostly of officers, their names on pieces of barrel staves or broken board, stuck in the dust.

Memoranda during the war: 21 December 1862

A Charge by Northern Troops in 1865

COME UP FROM THE FIELDS FATHER

Come up from the fields father, here's a letter from our
    Pete,
And come to the front door mother, here's a letter from
    thy dear son.

Lo, 'tis autumn,
Lo, where the trees, deeper green, yellower and redder,
Cool and sweeten Ohio's villages with leaves fluttering
    in the moderate wind,

Where apples ripe in the orchards hang and grapes on
    the trellis'd vines,
(Smell you the smell of the grapes on the vines?
Smell you the buckwheat where the bees were lately
    buzzing?)

Above all, lo, the sky so calm, so transparent after the
    rain, and with wondrous clouds,
Below too, all calm, all vital and beautiful, and the
    farm prospers well.

Down in the fields all prospers well,
But now from the fields come father, come at the
    daughter's call,
And come to the entry mother, to the front door come
    right away.

Fast as she can she hurries, something ominous, her
    steps trembling,
She does not tarry to smooth her hair nor adjust her cap.

Open the envelope quickly,
O this is not our son's writing, yet his name is sign'd,
O a strange hand writes for our dear son, O stricken
    mother's soul!

All swims before her eyes, flashes with black, she
    catches the main words only,
Sentences broken, *gunshot wound in the breast, cavalry
skirmish, taken to hospital,*
At present low, but will soon be better.

Ah now the single figure to me,
Amid all teeming and wealthy Ohio with all its cities
    and farms,
Sickly white in the face and dull in the head, very faint,
By the jamb of a door leans.

Grieve not so, dear mother, (the just-grown daughter
    speaks through her sobs,
The little sisters huddle around speechless and
    dismay'd,)
See, dearest mother, the letter says Pete will soon be better.

Alas poor boy, he will never be better, (nor may-be
    needs to be better, that brave and simple soul,)
While they stand at home at the door he is dead already,
The only son is dead.

But the mother needs to be better,
She with thin form presently drest in black,
By day her meals untouch'd, then at night fitfully
    sleeping, often waking,
In the midnight waking, weeping, longing with one
    deep longing,
O that she might withdraw unnoticed, silent from life
    escape and withdraw,
To follow, to seek, to be with her dear dead son.

WALT WHITMAN

CLOSE STUDY

1 Look at the descriptions of the Ohio countryside around the farm. Make a list of **adjectives**, **verbs** and **phrases** that describe its richness and fertility.

2 How exactly does the family receive the news of Pete and what does the message say?

3 Whitman focuses on the mother. Which lines and details show her nervous feelings and reactions to the news?

4 How do the reaction of the daughters add to the **pathos**?

5 Apart from family affections, why is his death so devastating to the farming family?

6 In the last section of the poem, pick out the words and phrases that movingly show the effect of Pete's death on the mother.

7 The poet uses **free verse** in this narrative poem. Comment on where it is most effective.

In another poem, Whitman wrote these lines about the battle dead.

> I saw battle corpses, myriads of them,
> And the white skeletons of young men – I saw them …
> But I saw they were not as was thought;
> They themselves were fully at rest – they suffered not;
> The living remained and suffered – the mother suffered,
> And the wife and the child, and the musing
>   comrade suffered ….

In what ways are these lines like the last section of *Come up from the Fields Father*?

✏ WRITING

1   Imagine that you are one of the family. Tell the story of the poem as a first person narrative. Include details of the farm and the beautiful countryside. Show the feelings and reactions of other members of the family, and include a memory of Pete in the form of a flashback.

2   Whitman contrasts peace and war – and sees the pathos and waste of the destruction of individuals in battle. Write about the poem, *Come up from the Fields Father*, outlining its story and showing how Whitman expresses his anti-war theme through:

   - pictures of the farm and the surrounding countryside
   - the effects of the bad news on members of the family

3   The first dramatic photographs of battle were taken during the American Civil War. Tell the story of this soldier (below), perhaps through the eyes of a close army friend. You could make him into Pete of the poem.

Dead Confederate soldier at Fredricksburg, 1863: photographed by Timothy O'Sullivan

The Civil War cost the lives of more than half a million men on the two sides. Bret Harte, a journalist and short story writer, found a strange new way to think about these deaths in a poem.

WHAT THE BULLET SANG

O joy of creation
　　To be!
O rapture to fly
　　And be free!
Be the battle lost or won,
Though its smoke shall hide the sun,
I shall find my love, – the one
　　Born for me!

I shall know him where he stands,
　　All alone,
With the power in his hands
　　Not o'erthrown;
I shall know him by his face,
By his godlike front and grace;
I shall hold him for a space,
　　All my own!

It is he – O my love!
　　So bold!
It is I – all thy love
　　Foretold!
It is I. O love! What bliss!
Dost thou answer to my kiss?
O sweetheart! What is this
　　Lieth there so cold?

BRET HARTE

🔍 CLOSE STUDY

This looks like a love poem but it is not.

1   What is it about?

2   Who is the 'speaker'?

3   Do you find the poem comic/sad/bitter/horrifying?

4   What is the point of these words:
   Born for me!
   …his godlike front and grace;
   What is this / Lieth there so cold? …?

5   Do you find the poem impressive or merely strange?

UNIT 4 //
Defending the Empire

Pride in the vast British Empire was an important part of the life and thought of late-Victorian Britain, not least in the great independent schools. There the men were raised who would rule and lead the fight to defend the overseas possessions. Latin and Greek were still the basis of study in these schools, and lessons from the writers of Rome were eagerly seized upon to guide the new Empire builders. The Roman poet Lucretius had such a message:

> Some nations grow and others fade and in a short space of time the generations of living things change and, like runners, hand on the torch of life ...

Henry Newbolt was the most patriotic poet of Britain's Empire. He borrowed Lucretius' idea to make the title of his 1892 poem, *Vitaï Lampada*: the torch of life. He begins with boys playing cricket in a public school. Then he sees them as men defending some outpost of Empire.

🔘 CLOSE STUDY

1   What is the boys' situation in the first stanza?

2   What is the Captain's message?

3   What is happening in the second stanza?

4   What is strange about the officer's call?

5   What message does Newbolt have for public school boys in the last stanza?

6   What exactly is the torch that they hand on?

7   How is war seen in this poem?

8   Do you find this poem exciting/memorable/outdated/ridiculous/inspiring?

9   Compare the poem to this passage from a famous war correspondent's report for the *Daily Mail*, describing Kitchener's army in the Sudan:

✏️ WRITING

Write a letter to Henry Newbolt telling him what you like and what you dislike about his poem and the ideas that it contains. Quote from the poem to support your points.

VITAÏ LAMPADA

There's a breathless hush in the Close tonight –
   Ten to make and the match to win –
A bumping pitch and a blinding light,
   An hour to play and the last man in.
And it's not for the sake of a ribboned coat,
   Or the selfish hope of a season's fame,
But his Captain's hand on his shoulder smote:
   'Play up! play up! and play the game!'

The sand of the desert is sodden red, –
   Red with the wreck of a square[1] that broke; –
The Gatling's[2] jammed and the Colonel dead,
   And the regiment blind with dust and smoke.
The river of death has brimmed his banks,
   And England's far, and Honour a name,
But the voice of a schoolboy rallies the ranks:
   'Play up! play up! and play the game!'

This is the word that year by year,
   While in her place the School is set,
Every one of her sons must hear,
   And none that hears it dare forget.
This they all with a joyful mind
   Bear through life like a torch in flame,
And falling fling to the host behind –
   'Play up! play up! and play the game!'

HENRY NEWBOLT

[1] *square: military formation*
[2] *Gatling: machine gun*

The bullets had whispered to raw youngsters in one breath the secret of all the glories of the British Army. ... Three men went down without a cry at the very foot of the Union Jack. ... The flag shook itself and still blazed splendidly ... don't look too much about you. Black spindle-legs curled up to meet red-gimleted black faces, donkeys headless and legless or sieves of shrapnel, camels ... rotting already in pools of blood ... heads without faces and faces without anything below ... don't look at it all. ... Once more, hurrah, hurrah, hurrah ...

George Steevens: *Daily Mail*, April 1898

Red-coated British soldiers fighting in Africa, 1879: George Fripp

Irish-born William Allingham had little sympathy for the battles of the British Empire.

In the nineteenth century, British forces fought two wars in Afghanistan to protect the North-West frontier of India. In this **sonnet** about the second war (1878-80), Allingham sees conquerors (red-coated British soldiers) and conquered (local tribesmen) as victims of British power.

In the **octet**, he asks someone secure in England (the mother) to imagine their fates as winter sweeps across the grim mountains of Afghanistan. In the **sestet**, he shows us the battle victim in the snow.

IN SNOW

O English mother, in the ruddy glow
Hugging your baby closer when outside
You see the silent, soft, and cruel snow
Falling again, and think what ills betide
Unshelter'd creatures, – your sad thoughts may go
Where War and Winter now, two spectre-wolves,
Hunt in the freezing vapour that involves
Those Asian peaks of ice and gulfs below.
Does this young soldier heed[1] the snow that fills
His mouth and open eyes? or mind, in truth,
To-night, his mother's parting syllables?
Ha! is't a red coat? – Merely blood. Keep ruth[2]
For others; this is but an Afghan youth
Shot by the stranger on his native hills.

WILLIAM ALLINGHAM

[1] **heed:** *notice*
[2] **ruth:** *pity*

1 Which words suggest the comfort and security of the 'English mother'?

2 Which **adjective** expresses the harshness of the world outside?

3 As she thinks about 'unsheltered creatures' suffering in winter, she imagines the distant war in Afghanistan. What **metaphor** conveys the deadly threats of war and winter for the soldier?

4 She focuses on one battle victim. What is sad about his face? Why would a mother feel strongly about him?

5 What is the grim idea about 'red coat' and 'blood'?

6 'Keep ruth for others' and 'This is but an Afghan youth': in these phrases, Allingham pretends not to care about the young man. What does he really think? Which two words tell you this?

UNIT 5 //

The Boer War 1899-1902

The Boer War began as a struggle between British and Dutch 'Boer' settlers for control of diamond and gold deposits in the Orange Free State and Transvaal provinces of South Africa. After early defeats, the British Army, reinforced by troops from other parts of the Empire, claimed victory in 1900. However, the Boers, who were great horse-riders and riflemen, continued fighting by using clever guerrilla tactics. Only when the British adopted a 'scorched earth' policy, whereby farms were burned and women and children were rounded up into 'concentration camps', did they finally crush the Boers.

The spread of education in the nineteenth century had produced a flood of popular newspapers and magazines. Poetry about the fighting in South Africa was a feature of these during the Boer War. There was some crude verse from soldiers but the most impressive poems came from war correspondents at the front or from civilians at home. As there was much opposition to the purpose and methods of the conflict, anti-war verse was a striking feature of this writing.

Thomas Hardy, already famous for his novels, wrote some of the best poems of the War. His powerful imagination allowed him to share the feelings and experiences of people more actively involved.

In his local Dorset newspaper, Hardy read of the death of a drummer boy, who was born in a village near Dorchester. He thought how sad it was that a boy, too young to understand the war, should be buried in an alien landscape so far from home. 'Hodge' was a nickname given at that time to the typical 'country bumpkin'. Hardy usually objected to the name but used it here to show the cruelty of war to the individual.

DRUMMER HODGE

They throw in Drummer Hodge, to rest
   Uncoffined – just as found:
His landmark is a kopje[1]-crest
   That breaks the veldt[2] around;
And foreign constellations west
   Each night above his mound.

Young Hodge the Drummer never knew –
   Fresh from his Wessex home –
The meaning of the broad Karoo[3],
   The Bush, the dusty loam,
And why uprose to nightly view
   Strange stars amid the gloam[4].

Yet portion of that unknown plain
   Will Hodge for ever be;
His homely Northern breast and brain
   Grow to some southern tree,
And strange-eyed constellations reign
     His stars eternally.

THOMAS HARDY

[1] **kopje:** *small hill*
[2] **veldt:** *open grassland*
[3] **karoo:** *dry grasslands*
[4] **gloam:** *evening*

CLOSE STUDY

1   What is the force of these words and phrases: 'They throw in ... uncoffined'?

2   What did Hodge never understand during his war service in South Africa?

3   Hardy uses several South African words. Why? What effect do they have on the **theme** of the poem?

4   Why does Hardy find Hodge's fate more strange than tragic?

5   What does Hardy mean in the last stanza by:

    His homely Northern breast and brain
    Grow to some southern tree, ?

Thomas Hardy's *A Wife in London* describes a lonely woman waiting nervously for news of her husband fighting in South Africa, the 'far South Land'. The poem is like a miniature version of one of Hardy's short stories. Those often depend on **irony**, which might be seen in Hardy's writing as grim jokes played on people by Fate. Hardy, with his strong sympathy for women, presents an oblique view of war's suffering, showing a victim thousands of miles from the fighting.

A WIFE IN LONDON

I

She sits in the tawny vapour[1]
    That the Thames-side lanes have uprolled,
    Behind whose webby fold on fold
Like a waning taper
    The street-lamp glimmers cold.

A messenger's knock cracks smartly,
    Flashed news[2] is in her hand
    Of meaning it dazes to understand
Though shaped so shortly:
    He-has fallen-in the far South Land. ...

II

'Tis the morrow; the fog hangs thicker,
    The postman nears and goes:
    A letter is brought whose lines disclose
By the firelight flicker
    His hand, whom the worm now knows:

Fresh – firm – penned in highest feather –
    Page-full of his hoped return,
    And of home-planned jaunts by brake and burn[3]
In the summer weather,
    And of new love that they would learn.

THOMAS HARDY

[1] **tawny vapour:** *yellow-brown fog*
[2] **flashed news:** *telegram*
[3] **brake and burn:** *thicket and stream*

British dead at Spion Kop, January 1900

1 What might the woman be thinking about in stanza 1?

2 Hardy liked **pathetic fallacy**, a trick of perception in which objects and landscapes seem to reflect our moods and thoughts. What do the fog and the street-lamp tell us about the woman's thinking?

3 What message is in the telegram?

4 What is its effect on her?

5 In part II a letter arrives. Who is it from and what does it say?

6 What does 'His hand, whom the worm now knows' means?

7 Hardy was always impressed by twists of fate in people's lives. What **ironies** can you see in this poem?

✏️ **WRITING**

In later life, the woman looks back on the sad episode of the telegram and the letter. Writing as 'I', record her memories, starting 'It was a foggy evening …' Include plenty of detail of the setting, and the irony of the letter's arrival. Add extra details to your story from this painting, *Boer War 1900* by John Byam Shaw.

A mourning wife: *Boer War 1900*: John Byam Shaw

Edgar Wallace was an army medical orderly in South Africa when the war began. Then he became a war correspondent for Reuters and the *Daily Mail*. His vivid Boer War poems, *Writ in barracks*, appeared in 1900.

The poem is set in an emergency field hospital near the front line. A battle is going on in the distance. A doctor is doing the best he can to help casualties. A badly wounded man with a massive injury caused by a ricochet is brought in.

WAR

I

A tent that is pitched at the base:
    A wagon that comes from the night:
A stretcher – and on it a Case:
    A surgeon, who's holding a light,
The Infantry's bearing the brunt –
    O hark to the wind-carried cheer!
A mutter of guns at the front:
    A whimper of sobs at the rear.
And it's *War*! 'Orderly, hold the light.
    You can lay him down on the table: so.
Easily – gently! Thanks – you may go.'
    And it's *War*! but the part that is not for show.

II

A tent, with a table athwart,
    A table that's laid out for one;
A waterproof cover – and nought
    But the limp, mangled work of a gun.
A bottle that's stuck by the pole,
    A guttering dip in its neck;
The flickering light of a soul
    On the wondering eyes of The Wreck[1],
And it's *War*! 'Orderly, hold his hand.
    I'm not going to hurt you, so don't be afraid.
A ricochet![2] God! What a mess it has made!'
    And it's *War*! and a very unhealthy trade.

III

The clink of a stopper and glass:
    A sigh as the chloroform drips:
A trickle of – what? on the grass,
    And bluer and bluer the lips.
The lashes have hidden the stare …
    A rent, and the clothes fall away …
A touch, and the wound is laid bare …
    A cut, and the face has turned grey …
And it's *War*! 'Orderly, take It out.
    It's hard for his child, and it's rough on his wife.
There might have been – sooner – a chance for his life
    But it's *War*! And – Orderly, clean this knife!'

EDGAR WALLACE

[1] **The Wreck**: *wounded man*
[2] **ricochet**: *bullet that rebounds off another surface*

◉ CLOSE STUDY

1 Wallace tells us what the orderly *hears* as well as what he sees. Which sounds add to the drama and **atmosphere** of the first stanza?

2 What does he mean by '*War! but the part that is not for show*'?

3 Comment on what you find striking about the description of the setting and the patient in the second stanza. What is significant about the table and the candle, for instance?

4 Select all the details from the third stanza that show the careful observation and which bring the scene to life for the reader.

5 Why is '*It*', said by the doctor, such a shocking word here?

6 Where in stanzas 2 and 3 does the doctor show sympathy for the battle victim?

7 What is the effect of these quotations:
... *a very unhealthy trade.*
'*Orderly, clean this knife!*'?

8 Make a list of words that begin lines in this poem. Do you like this style? Where is it most effective?

✎ WRITING

The orderly writes to a friend about the incident. Compose the letter, describing the events and atmosphere, and the feelings that the orderly had at the time. How does he feel about it now?

Start your piece like this:

> Every day that I work in the field hospital makes me feel more lucky to be alive and well. Some of the cases I see ....

Saving the Guns at Colenso: 15th December 1899: Stanley Berkeley

Rudyard Kipling, who was already world-famous as a poet and novelist, went to South Africa as a journalist during the Boer War. Usually he was a devoted supporter of the military and the British Empire but he had moments of grave doubt as he watched the effects of the fighting.

Bloemfontein, a Boer stronghold in the Orange Free State, was captured by the British in March 1900. Kipling stayed there, helping to run *The Friend*, a paper for the troops. Typhoid fever broke out in the overcrowded town. Soon there were more than ten deaths a day. The few women volunteer nurses, called from England, themselves began to die. Their courage and endurance are the subjects of *Dirge of Dead Sisters*, from which these stanzas are an extract.

---

from: DIRGE OF DEAD SISTERS[1]
(For the nurses who died in the South African War)

Who recalls the twilight and the ranged tents in order
  (Violet peaks uplifted through the crystal evening air?)
And the clink of iron teacups and the piteous, noble laughter,
  And the faces of the Sisters with the dust upon their hair?

Who recalls the noontide and the funerals through the
  market,
  (Blanket-hidden bodies, flagless, followed by the flies?)
And the footsore firing-party, and the dust and stench and
  staleness,
  And the faces of the Sisters and the glory in their eyes?

(Bold behind the battle, in the open camp all-hallowed[2],
  Patient, wise, and mirthful in the ringed[3] and reeking town,
These endured unresting till they rested from their labours –
  Little wasted bodies, ah, so light to lower down!) …

RUDYARD KIPLING

[1] **dirge:** *a mournful song, sung to lament the dead*
[2] **hallowed:** *blessed*
[3] **ringed:** *surrounded by the enemy*

CLOSE STUDY

Stanza 1

1 Which details create a striking picture of the landscape?

2 Why is the nurses' laughter 'piteous and noble'?

3 Why is it sad to remember the women's hair covered in dust?

Stanza 2

4 What ceremony attends the victims' funerals?

5 Which words and phrases make the funerals seem ugly and pointless?

6 How do the nurses contrast with their ugly surroundings?

Stanza 3

7 The town is 'ringed' (surrounded by Boer enemies) and 'reeking' (there is little sanitation). In this grim place, what fine qualities do the nurses show in their work?

8 How are they treated by the soldiers?

9 How do the nurses 'rest from their labours'?

10 Why is 'light', in the last line, so sad?

11 The **rhythm** of this poem is captivating. Can you trace the unusual **meter**? Which lines are most impressive in this respect?

12 Describe the **mood** of the poem extract. Consider the effect created by starting stanzas with the words 'Who recalls…'.

WRITING

Imagine that Kipling wrote a report on these nurses for a London newspaper, to highlight the humanity found amidst warfare. Write his report mentioning their appearance and brave qualities, and, sometimes, their sad fate. Include a description of their war surroundings in Bloemfontein.

In *The Hyaenas*, Kipling, reflecting on what he had observed in India and South Africa, notes how these ugly scavengers would dig up and eat buried soldiers. This is their instinct and he does not blame them. His real target of anger is seen in the bitter concluding lines.

THE HYAENAS

After the burial-parties leave
    And the baffled kites[1] have fled;
The wise hyaenas come out at eve
    To take account of our dead.

How he died and why he died
    Troubles them not a whit[2].
They snout the bushes and stones aside
    And dig till they come to it.

They are only resolute they shall eat
    That they and their mates may thrive,
And they know the dead are safer meat
    Than the weakest thing alive.

(For a goat may butt, and a worm may sting,
    And a child will sometimes stand;
But a poor dead soldier of the King
    Can never lift a hand.)

They whoop and halloo and scatter the dirt
    Until their tushes[3] white
Take good hold in the army shirt,
    And tug the corpse to light,

And the pitiful face is shewn again
    For an instant ere they close;
But it is not discovered to living men –
    Only to God and to those

Who, being soulless, are free from shame,
    Whatever meat they may find.
Nor do they defile the dead man's name –
    That is reserved for his kind[4].

RUDYARD KIPLING

[1] **kites:** *birds of prey*
[2] **a whit:** *a bit*
[3] **tushes:** *pointed teeth*
[4] **his kind:** *human beings*

CLOSE STUDY

1   Which words and phrases express horror at the hyaenas and their behaviour?

2   Which show a kind of understanding of them?

3   What is the force of the first two lines of the second stanza?

4   Find the phrases that describe the dead soldier. Which is most upsetting?

5   What is the effect of the **comparisons** with the dead body in the fourth stanza?

6   The hyaenas eat the dead man. They do not defile him by not caring for him in camp (thousands of men died of disease), by setting him impossible tasks or by blaming him for defeat. His 'kind' do these. Exactly what sort of people is Kipling thinking of here?

7   Trace the forceful **rhymes** of this poem. Where does Kipling use them with most power?

WRITING

1   Write about the poem and how Kipling has used the hyaenas to make a powerful statement about the inhumanity of war. Describe the setting of the soldier's burial. What horrible things do the hyaenas do with the dead man? How does Kipling feel about them? What is the angry message of the poem's conclusion?

2   Re-read all four Boer War poems – *A Wife in London*, *War*, *Dirge of Dead Sisters*, *The Hyaenas*. Write about them, showing what they tell us about the pity of war. Explain each story and setting, the messages given by the poets and anything else that interests you in the language and style.

UNIT 6 //

Voices prophesying war

In the early years of the twentieth century, the possibility of a war in Europe was much discussed. The continent became divided by great alliances: Britain, France and Russia against Germany and Austria-Hungary. Large armies were built up and battle plans worked out. There were flash points in the Balkans and colonial rivalries which increased the tension.

Written in 1894, William Watson's amazingly prophetic sonnet, *The world in armour*, drew an ominous picture of Europe's coming fate. He has three visions of the future, each of which **personifies** Europe as a young woman.

The War, by Arnold Bocklin (1896), shows the Four Horsemen of the Apocalypse - violence, famine, disease, and death - who represent symbolically the effects of war.

THE WORLD IN ARMOUR

A moment's fantasy, the vision came
Of Europe dipped in fiery death, and so
Mounting re-born, with vestal[1] limbs aglow,
Splendid and fragrant from her bath of flame.
It fleeted[2]; and a phantom without name,
Sightless, dismembered, terrible, said: "Lo,
I am that ravished Europe men shall know
After the morn of blood and night of shame."

The spectre passed, and I beheld alone
The Europe of the present, as she stands,
Powerless from terror of her own vast power,
'Neath novel stars, beside a brink[3] unknown;
And round her the sad Kings[4], with sleepless hands,
Piling the faggots[5], hour by doomful hour.

WILLIAM WATSON

[1] **vestal:** *chaste*
[2] **fleeted:** *passed quickly*
[3] **brink:** *edge of the sea*
[4] **Kings:** *rulers of Europe*
[5] **faggots:** *bundles of wood*

● CLOSE STUDY

1   Look at the first four lines. Some people thought that war would revitalize European countries, and get rid of old ideas and ways of government. How is that hope represented in the **metaphor** of the 'bath of flame' (war)?

2   In the next four lines, a second terrible vision shows that war may be purely destructive. How is Europe seen here?

3   In the sonnet's **sestet**, Watson returns to his own time. Europe is standing on the edge of an unknown sea: the future. What are the 'Kings' (the rulers of the various countries) doing?

4   What is represented by the 'faggots'?

5   Look at the **adjectives**: 'sad', 'sleepless', and 'doomful'. What is the force of each?

6   What do you find impressive about this strange **sonnet**?

Battleships, that are testing their guns in Thomas Hardy's *Channel Firing*, were the most impressive weapon systems before 1914. Britain and Germany were caught in a deadly race to produce more of these 'floating steel castles'.

Hardy published this poem in May 1914 and came to see it as prophetic of the 'Red war' that started four months later.

◉ CLOSE STUDY

1 'We' are the dead men buried around the church. Why do they sit up?

2 What other effects do the battleship guns have on the village?

3 What impression of God do you get in this poem?

4 How does he describe the state of the world to the dead men?

5 What conclusions do the skeletons come to after God's message to them?

6 The three places in the last two lines are connected with former British civilizations that fought for a time and finally lost. Why include them in this poem?

7 Is this poem comic/serious/frightening? Do you think it is out-of-date, or has it something to tell us about our world?

CHANNEL FIRING

That night your great guns, unawares,
Shook all our coffins as we lay,
And broke the chancel window-squares,
We thought it was the Judgement-day

And sat upright. While drearisome
Arose the howl of wakened hounds:
The mouse let fall the altar-crumb,
The worms drew back into the mounds,

The glebe[1] cow drooled. Till God called, 'No;
It's gunnery practice out at sea
Just as before you went below;
The world is as it used to be:

'All nations striving strong to make
Red war yet redder. Mad as hatters
They do no more for Christés sake
Than you who are helpless in such matters.

'That is not the judgement-hour
For some of them's a blessed thing,
For if it were they'd have to scour[2]
Hell's floor for so much threatening …

'Ha, ha. It will be warmer when
I blow the trumpet[3] (if indeed
I ever do; for you are men,
And rest eternal sorely need).'

So down we lay again, 'I wonder,
Will the world ever saner be,'
Said one, 'than when He sent us under
In our indifferent century!'

And many a skeleton shook his head,
'Instead of preaching forty year,'
My neighbour Parson Thirdly said,
'I wish I had stuck to pipes and beer.'

Again the guns disturbed the hour,
Roaring their readiness to avenge,
As far inland as Stourton Tower[4],
And Camelot[5], and starlit Stonehenge.

THOMAS HARDY

[1] *glebe: church-owned field*
[2] *scour: scrub*
[3] *blow the trumpet: Day of Judgement*
[4] *Stourton Tower: monument to King Alfred's victory over the Danes in 879*
[5] *Camelot: legendary castle of King Arthur*

1 Write your own verse sketch, based loosely on the ideas of Hardy's poem. The dead are again awoken by war-like sounds of today (aircraft, perhaps) and question you about war and peace in the twenty-first century.

2 Look at the painting *Apocalyptic Landscape* by a German artist, Ludwig Meidner. One of a series produced in what he called the 'angry, vicious, doom-laden' summer of 1913, it is a dramatic prophecy of what would happen to cities amid war in the twentieth century. It could be a Belgian city in 1914, 1940 London, 1945 Berlin or Baghdad in 2003. Write a short imaginative description based on this amazing picture.

> So the attack had come at last!
> How fantastic it all was in a
> complicated, modern city.
> Around me I could see...

Or your piece could be a poem about cities in war in the twentieth and twenty-first centuries.

City war of the future: *Apocalyptic landscape* (1913): Ludwig Meidner

PART 2

THE FIRST WORLD WAR 1914–18

Repelling a German Counter-Attack by Frank Dadd, shows typical 1914–18 warfare with heavy infantry losses during attacks on lines defended by barbed wire and machine guns

Introduction

In 1914, Europe was divided by two great alliances: Britain and her Empire, France, Russia, Serbia and Italy against Germany, Austria-Hungary and Turkey. Tensions – based on political, military and colonial rivalries – had been rising since 1900. Balkan terrorists created a flash point at Sarajevo in Bosnia in June 1914. By August, Europe was at war.

On the Eastern Front, Germany and Austria fought savagely against Russia, which collapsed into revolution in 1917. On the Western Front, heavily defended trench lines produced deadlock. Nightmarish battles of 'attrition', like Verdun and the Somme (1916) and Ypres (1917), caused massive casualties. The Germans broke the Western Front in March 1918, but the brilliantly planned Anglo-French counter-attack finally defeated the Germans in November 1918.

The fighting was tenacious and fierce to the end. 'There was no forgiveness in any combatant nation in Europe,' wrote Philip Gibbs, a journalist. 'Like wolves they had their teeth in each others' throats, and would not let go, though all bloody and exhausted.' The Central Powers lost three and a half million men; the Allies over five million. On average, 5,600 combatants were killed on each day of the Great War. Millions more were crippled, maimed or disfigured, or broken by 'shell-shock'.

Oppy Wood 1917 evening: John Nash

WAR POETRY 1914-18

The fashion for war poetry of the Boer war era was revived in 1914. The press was once again filled with poems, often used to stimulate recruiting or to comment on war news. Most of the early war poetry was very bad.

> ## from: SONG IN WAR-TIME
>
> At the sound of the drum
> Out of their dens they come, they come,
> The little poets we hoped were dumb
> The little poets we hoped were dead
> The poets who certainly haven't been read
> Since heaven knows when, they come,
> they come,
> At the sound of the drum, of the drum,
> of the drum …
>
> *HERBERT BLENHEIM*
> from *The Egoist:* 1914

The death of Rupert Brooke and the craze for his war sonnets began a second fashion for 'soldier poets'. Many young officers strung together verses about Honour, Duty, and Sacrifice. As these men fell in battle, proud parents published these 'poems' in slim volumes.

> *Lying about in every smart London drawing-room, you would find the latest little volume, and at every fashionable bookshop the half-crown war poets were among the best selling lines … No doubt the ghoulish traffic in the verse exercises of dead schoolboys was an excellent business proposition …*

Douglas Goldring: from *Reputations* 1920

The grandly vague style of the poems was made fun of by a famous critic:

> *They turn out their works on a formula. Put England down as "knightly", state her honour to be "inviolate" … introduce a "thou" or two, and conclude with the assertion that God will defend the Right — and there's the formula for a poem.*

A third wave of war poetry – by Wilfred Owen, Siegfried Sassoon and others – is that which is now remembered and admired. Owen resented the fake 'heroes' who were invented in early war verse. He wanted to tell the truth about the real heroism and suffering that he had seen in France. Sassoon also wished to tell the public about the Western Front, the 'hell where youth and laughter go.' He spoke up for the courage and endurance of

> The unreturning army that was youth;
> The legions who have suffered and are dust.
>
> from *Prelude: The troops*

UNIT 7 //

Recruiting poems

When war began in August 1914, Britain, unlike other European powers which had huge conscript armies, relied only on a small professional force. Lord Kitchener, Secretary of State for War, saw that the conflict would be long and hard fought, and proposed a revolutionary plan for 'New Armies' of millions of volunteers. His own grim face, over the slogan 'Your King and Country Need You', appeared in the first poster appeal for recruits. Until conscription was introduced in 1916, young men were subjected to relentless social pressures, both official and unofficial, to join the army.

Newspapers of all kinds gave space to recruiting poems. Harold Begbie's *Fall In*, which first appeared in the *Daily Chronicle* on 31 August 1914, became tremendously popular. It was set to music and sung in music halls; posters and badges related to the poem were produced: 'Sing the Song! Wear the badge! Play the March!'

Recruiting poster

FALL IN

What will you lack, sonny, what will you lack
  When the girls line up the street,
Shouting their love to the lads come back
  From the foe they rushed to beat?
Will you send a strangled cheer to the sky
  And grin till your cheeks are red?
But what will you lack when your mate goes by
  With a girl who cuts you dead?[1]

Where will you look, sonny, where will you look
  When your children yet to be
Clamour to learn of the part you took
  In the War that kept men free?
Will you say it was naught to you if France
  Stood up to her foe or bunked?
But where will you look when they give you the glance
  That tells you they know you funked?

How will you fare, sonny, how will you fare
  In the far-off winter night,
When you sit by the fire in an old man's chair
  And your neighbours talk of the fight?
Will you slink away, as it were from a blow,
  Your old head shamed and bent?
Or, say – I was not with the first to go,
  But I went, thank God, I went?

Why do they call, sonny, why do they call
  For men, who are brave and strong?
Is it naught to you if your country fall,
  And Right is smashed by Wrong?
Is it football still and the picture show,
  The pub and the betting odds,
When your brothers stand to the tyrant's blow
  And Britain's call is God's?

HAROLD BEGBIE

[1] **cuts you dead:** *ignores you*

🖉 CLOSE STUDY

1 Begbie tries to make 'shirkers' feel ashamed of not volunteering. Each **stanza** proposes a different key point. What are these four points? Which would be most persuasive for young men?

2 The simple rhymed lines are clear and memorable. Which line in each stanza has most force?

3 Suppose that you could argue with Begbie. What answers would you give to his points?

J.A. Nicklin was a teacher and writer whose little book *And they went to war* (1914), gave us poem portraits of various kinds of volunteer in Kitchener's army.

THE CITY CLERK

" We were sick to death of ledger[1] and of day book,
  Bored to death in City and on 'Change;[2]
For us at tea-time Lyons'[3] Peggy may look;
  We're taking tea with Prussians –at long range.

"We'd had enough of 'footer' and of cricket;
  But what bowling and what charges we have seen
Since we started out to keep up England's wicket
  And to give and take War's passes, sharp and clean!

"When the air with hurtling shrapnel's all a-quiver
  And the smoke of battle through the valley swirls,
It's better than our Sundays up the river,
  And the rifle's hug is closer than a girl's."

J.A.NICKLIN

[1] **ledger:** *account book*
[2] **'Change:** *the Royal Exchange*
[3] **Lyons:** *popular café*

🖉 CLOSE STUDY

1 What did the clerks find dull about their peacetime lives?

2 Why is war better?

3 How are sport and going out with girls related to war?

4 The poet Edward Thomas particularly liked the last two lines of this sketch. What makes them vivid?

Jessie Pope was a popular journalist. She wrote war poems, to help recruiting and to sustain the war effort, for the *Daily Mail* and *Daily Express*. Journalism was one of the first professions open to women, and Jessie Pope made a good living from her prolific writing that reflected popular attitudes of her time. She has become notorious to us because Wilfred Owen addressed the first draft of *Dulce et decorum est* to her (see p.77). There she is 'my friend', the typical unfeeling civilian enjoying the drama and supposed glamour of war, and helping to force men to fight.

WHO'S FOR THE GAME?

Who's for the game, the biggest that's played,
  The red crashing game of a fight?
Who'll grip and tackle the job unafraid?
  And who thinks he'd rather sit tight?

Who'll toe the line for the signal to 'Go!'?
  Who'll give his country a hand?
Who wants a turn to himself in the show?
  And who wants a seat in the stand?

Who knows it won't be a picnic – not much –
  Yet eagerly shoulders a gun?
Who would much rather come back with a crutch
  Than lie low and be out of the fun?

Come along, lads – but you'll come on all right –
  For there's only one course to pursue,
Your country is up to her neck in a fight,
  And she's looking and calling for you.

JESSIE POPE

CLOSE STUDY

The poem aims to make young men join the army. To do this, she compares war to sport: it is a new way to 'play for England'.

1   Which words and phrases build this **comparison**?

2   What do you think of the poet's phrases: 'rather come back with a crutch' and '…out of the fun'?

3   The poem uses **colloquial** language. List various examples of this and explain their effect. You will need to consider the **attitude** they convey and the **purpose** of the poem.

4   Like any good journalist, Pope had the knack of writing striking lines, that are impressive and grand-sounding. Find three such lines in *Who's for the Game?*

5   Comment on:
   • Pope's use of questions
   • the poem's **rhythm**.

I shouted for blood (1916) might be called an anti-recruiting poem. It is by the daughter of Harold Begbie (author of *Fall In*). As convinced Christians, both became revolted by the relentless slaughter (see p.84).

I SHOUTED FOR BLOOD

I shouted for blood as I ran, brother,
  Till my bayonet pierced your breast;
I lunged thro' the heart of a man, brother,
  That the sons of men might rest.

I swung up my rifle apace, brother,
  Gasping for breath awhile,
And I smote at your writhing face, brother,
  That the face of peace might smile.

Your eyes are beginning to glaze, brother,
  Your wounds are ceasing to bleed.
God's ways are wonderful ways, brother,
  And hard for your wife to read.

JANET BEGBIE

CLOSE STUDY

1   List the violent words that express the ferocity of the fighting.

2   The last lines of the first two **stanzas** give the soldier's motives for killing his 'brother', the enemy. What are they?

3   What do the last two lines tell us about Begbie's real feelings about war?

COMPARING POEMS

Compare this poem with *Who's for the Game?* Think about

• theme
• style
• imagery
• key words
• the message of each poem

RECRUITING

'Lads, you're wanted, go and help.'
On the railway carriage wall
Stuck the poster, and I thought
Of the hands that penned the call.

Fat civilians wishing they
'Could go out and fight the Hun'.
Can't you see them thanking God
That they're over forty-one?

Girls with feathers,[1] vulgar songs –
Washy verse on England's need –
God – and don't we damned well know
How the message ought to read.

'Lads, you're wanted! over there,'
Shiver in the morning dew,
More poor devils like yourselves
Waiting to be killed by you.

Go and help to swell the names
In the casualty lists.
Help to make the column's stuff
For the blasted journalists.

Help to keep them nice and safe
From the wicked German foe.
Don't let him come over here!
'Lads, you're wanted – out you go.'

*   *   *   *   *

There's a better word than that,
Lads, and can't you hear it come
From a million men that call
You to share their martyrdom?

Leave the harlots still to sing
Comic songs about the Hun,
Leave the fat old men to say
Now *we've* got them on the run.

Better twenty honest years
Than their dull three score and ten.
Lads, you're wanted. Come and learn
To live and die with honest men.

You shall learn what men can do
If you will but pay the price,
Learn the gaiety and strength
In the gallant sacrifice.

Take your risk of life and death
Underneath the open sky.
Live clean or go out quick –
Lads, you're wanted. Come and die.

E.A. MACKINTOSH

[1] *girls with feathers: some women gave white feathers*
to 'cowards' who were not in uniform.

E.A. Mackintosh left Oxford University to volunteer.
He was a gallant soldier, who won the Military
Cross, and was gassed and wounded at the Battle of
the Somme. He was killed at Cambrai in 1917. His
battle experience made him cynical about recruiting
posters and their slogans.

CLOSE STUDY

1   The poet sees a recruiting poster. It makes him
    think of aspects of life in war-time Britain that
    he detests. What are these?

2   Who are the 'poor devils' in the fourth stanza?

3   The words 'over there' make the poet reflect
    that he intensely admires and respects certain
    things about the soldiers in France and Flanders.
    What are these things?

1   Write your own recruiting poem in the style of the 1914 writers. You have to make war sound glamorous, exciting and manly.

2   Write a short story based on this photograph. The young man has volunteered for the army and is about to leave for war service abroad. Imagine the thoughts of each of the people in the picture, which probably mix pride, excitement and sadness. Write a paragraph about each person. Then add another expressing your own thoughts, or imagining the fate of the soldier.

1   Look carefully at the recruiting posters opposite. Discuss them together. What is the message of each? How do they attempt to persuade men into the army? Which is most effective?

2   Draw, or produce using ICT, your own recruiting poster with a good slogan (you will find lots more examples at www.firstworldwar.com/index.htm). Alternatively, devise an anti-war poster and slogan. Write a short persuasive speech to match your poster, selecting your language and using **rhetorical devices** to appeal to your listeners.

A soldier's goodbye photographed by F.J. Mortimer, 1914

The Kaiser's ambition to rule the world

In May 1915, the British liner Lusitania was sunk by a German U-boat off the Irish coast and 2000 people, including many women and children, were drowned.

UNIT 8 //
Ideals and chivalry

In 1914, most British people had forgotten what war was actually like. There had not been a major European conflict for a century. Only professional soldiers had fought in South Africa. Young men were restless. To us, the Edwardian era may seem attractive but to people of the time it was stuffy and dull, and also shameful with its strikes, suffragette riots, and its extremes of wealth and poverty. In August 1914, the war seemed a glorious adventure.

Poets reflected this enthusiasm. They showed the war as an epic. Honour, Glory, Sacrifice were key words. Ideals of chivalry, the old code of medieval knights, were taken from Victorian writers and painters who had loved the stories of King Arthur. A soldier was now a 'warrior'; the enemy the 'foe'. The dead were the 'fallen'; fighting was 'strife'. 'Guerdon', a knight's reward for service, was often used. Here is a selection of such poems, some of them much admired in their day.

Herbert Asquith, son of the Prime Minister, was badly wounded in battle. He wrote this poem a year or two before the war, but published it on 8 August 1914, when it became famous.

◉ CLOSE STUDY

1   What was the clerk's pre-war life like?

2   What did he dream about at his desk?

3   Describe his experience of war and what happened to him.

4   How does Asquith feel about the clerk's fate?

5   Pick out the **archaisms** in this poem. Why does the poet choose this **style**?

6   Do you like the **ideals** of this poem?

Rupert Brooke volunteered for the Royal Naval Division (marines) in August 1914, and saw brief service at Antwerp, Belgium in October. Back in camp in November, he wrote a set of five war **sonnets**. *Peace*, catching the heroic mood of the war's outbreak, is the first. Its opening echoes Shakespeare's *Henry V*: 'Now all the youth of England are on fire!' It claims that war brings excitement and purpose to young men's lives.

THE VOLUNTEER

Here lies a clerk who half his life had spent
Toiling at ledgers in a city grey,
Thinking that so his days would drift away
With no lance broken in life's tournament.
Yet ever 'twixt the books and his bright eyes
The gleaming eagles of the legions came,
And horsemen, charging under phantom skies,
Went thundering past beneath the oriflamme.[1]

And now those waiting dreams are satisfied;
From twilight to the halls of dawn he went;
His lance is broken; but he lies content
With that high hour, in which he lived and died.
And falling thus he wants no recompense,
Who found his battle in the last resort;
Nor need he any hearse to bear him hence,
Who goes to join the men of Agincourt.[2]

HERBERT ASQUITH

[1] **oriflamme:** *banner*
[2] **Agincourt:** *Henry V's victory in France, 1415*

PEACE

Now, God be thanked Who has matched us with His hour,
And caught our youth, and wakened us from sleeping,
With hand made sure, clear eye, and sharpened power,
To turn, as swimmers into cleanness leaping,
Glad from a world grown old and cold and weary,
Leave the sick hearts that honour could not move,
And half-men, and their dirty songs and dreary,
And all the little emptiness of love!

Oh! we, who have known shame, we have found release there,
Where there's no ill, no grief, but sleep has mending,
Naught broken save this body, lost but breath;
Nothing to shake the laughing heart's long peace there
But only agony, and that has ending;
And the worst friend and enemy is but Death.

RUPERT BROOKE

● CLOSE STUDY

Octet

1   Why do the young men of 1914 feel lucky?

2   How has the coming of war changed them?

3   Which unfavourable words describe the life of peacetime?

4   Comment on the effectiveness of the two **comparisons** used to express the excitement of volunteering for war.

Sestet

1   Which words and phrases tell you that Brooke seems unconcerned about wounds and death?

2   In contrast to these dangers is the contentment, 'the laughing heart's long peace', that comes from dutiful service to Britain in war. How then do you explain the title?

The last of the five sonnets, *The Soldier*, is the best known. Both poem and poet became hugely famous when it was read in St Paul's Cathedral on Easter Sunday, 1915, two weeks before Brooke died of blood poisoning on a troopship carrying him to the Gallipoli campaign in Turkey. Winston Churchill, Brooke's friend, noted that in the sonnets 'A voice had become audible, a note had been struck, more true, more thrilling, more able to do justice to the nobility of our youth in arms than any other'.

THE SOLDIER

If I should die, think only this of me:
  That there's some corner of a foreign field
That is for ever England. There shall be
  In that rich earth a richer dust concealed;
A dust whom England bore, shaped, made aware,
  Gave, once, her flowers to love, her ways to roam,
A body of England's, breathing English air,
  Washed by the rivers, blest by suns of home.

And think, this heart, all evil shed away,
  A pulse in the eternal mind, no less
    Gives somewhere back the thoughts by England given;
Her sights and sounds; dreams happy as her day;
And laughter, learnt of friends; and gentleness,
    In hearts at peace, under an English heaven.

RUPERT BROOKE

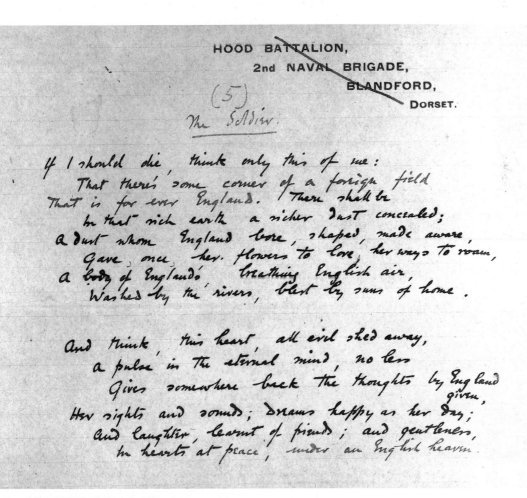

Manuscript of *The soldier* by Rupert Brooke.

Brooke loved to experiment with the sonnet, one of the great forms of English poetry. Compare *The Soldier* to *Peace*. Comment on

• attitudes to death in battle
• contrasts of peace and war
• landscape, life and values of England
• feeling of patriotism
• use of the sonnet form

✏️ **WRITING**

Imagine that Brooke writes a letter to a friend, explaining how he feels about entering the army in 1914. Write the letter, using ideas from both poems. Try to capture the confident mood of the poems.

Dulce et decorum appeared in *Punch* magazine in January 1916. Glasgow, like Wilfred Owen, took her Latin title from a line by the Roman poet Horace (p.77). Owen may have seen her poem: he certainly read *Punch*. Glasgow may have been included in his sarcastic address 'To Jessie Pope, etc' in his manuscript draft (p.78). She probably borrowed her goblet and sword imagery from Victorian paintings.

from: **DULCE ET DECORUM**[1]

All life was sweet – veiled mystery in its smile;
   High in your hands you held the brimming cup;[2]
Love waited at your bidding for a while,
   Not yet the time to take its challenge up;
Across the sunshine came no faintest breath
To whisper of the tragedy of death.

And then, beneath the soft and shining blue,
   Faintly you heard the drum's insistent beat;
The echo of its urgent note you knew,
   The shaken earth that told of marching feet;
With quickened breath you heard your country's call,
And from your hands you let the goblet[3] fall.

You snatched the sword, and answered as you went,
   For fear your eager feet should be outrun,
And with the flame of your bright youth unspent
   Went shouting up the pathway to the sun.
O valiant dead, take comfort where you lie.
So sweet to live?   Magnificent to die!

GERALDINE ROBERTSON GLASGOW

[1] *dulce et decorum est pro patria mori:*
   it is sweet and fitting to die for your country
[2] **cup:** *of life*
[3] **goblet:** *decorated cup*

🔍 **CLOSE STUDY**

1 What **symbol** is used for life in **stanza** one?

2 What great feature of life will the young man lose by dying in battle?

3 How is the declaration of war described in stanza two?

4 What **comparison** is used to describe the young man joining the army?

5 Why is it 'magnificent to die'?

6 Do you like the ideas of this poem? Or are they simply unrealistic?

📁 **COMPARING POEMS**

Compare this poem with Wilfred Owen's *Dulce et decorum est* (p.77). Consider

• the picture of the soldier victim
• the message of each poem
• the use of the Latin words
• diction and imagery in each poem

John McCrae was a Canadian doctor who wrote this poem at a dressing-station for the wounded near Ypres in 1915. His poem saw a link between the dead and the poppies that grew on their graves. After the war, this gave rise to the poppy symbol that is still used on Remembrance Day. McCrae himself died in 1918.

IN FLANDERS FIELDS

In Flanders fields the poppies blow
Between the crosses, row on row
   That mark our place; and in the sky
   The larks, still bravely singing, fly
Scarce heard amid the guns below.

We are the Dead. Short days ago
We lived, felt dawn, saw sunset glow,
   Loved and were loved, and now we lie
      In Flanders fields.

Take up our quarrel with the foe:
To you from failing hands we throw
   The torch; be yours to hold it high.
   If ye break faith with us who die
We shall not sleep, though poppies grow
      In Flanders fields.

JOHN McCRAE

CLOSE STUDY

1   How does the poet contrast life and death in the first two verses?

2   The dead speak. How do they remember life?

3   What is their message to other living soldiers?

Deeply moved by the destruction of the younger generation, Laurence Binyon wrote these well-known lines on the cliffs in Cornwall in late August 1914. The poem was published in *The Times* on 21 September. The second stanza in this extract is often quoted on Remembrance Day or is carved on war memorials. Binyon, an expert on Far-Eastern art at the British Museum, gave up his wartime leaves to work as a Red Cross orderly in France.

from: FOR THE FALLEN

They went with songs to the battle, they were young,
Straight of limb, true of eye, steady and aglow.
They were staunch to the end against odds uncounted:
They fell with their faces to the foe.

They shall grow not old, as we that are left grow old:
Age shall not weary them, nor the years condemn.
At the going down of the sun and in the morning
We will remember them.

LAURENCE BINYON

CLOSE STUDY

1   What good qualities does he see in the young soldiers?

2   What does 'faces to the foe' mean?

3   How do they remain in the minds of the survivors?

4   What, by contrast, happens to the survivors?

5   Do you like the old-fashioned words? Why does Binyon use them?

6   The poem is so familiar that it is hard to see it freshly. What do you think of these lines from *For the Fallen* and their message?

Robert Nichols was shell-shocked at the Somme in 1916. This is a sketch of the ruined battlefield.

DAWN ON THE SOMME

Last night rain fell over the scarred plateau,
And now from the dark horizon, dazzling, flies
Arrow on fire-plumed arrow to the skies,
Shot from the bright arc of Apollo's[1] bow;
And from the wild and writhen[2] waste below,
From flashing pools and mounds lit one by one,
Oh, is it mist, or are these companies
Of morning heroes who arise, arise
With thrusting arms, with limbs and hair aglow,
Toward the risen god, upon whose brow
Burns the gold laurel of all victories,
Hero and heroes' god, th' invincible Sun?

ROBERT NICHOLS

[1] **Apollo:** *ancient Greek idea that the sun was a god*
[2] **writhen:** *smashed and twisted*

CLOSE STUDY

1   Sunrise makes the morning mists rise. What **comparisons** does this create in the poet's mind?

2   Do you find these comparisons moving or artificial?

WRITING

1   Write about some or all of this group of poems, saying how the poets see:

   • soldiers in battle
   • death in war
   • war itself

Consider some of the comparisons and old-fashioned words that are used by the poets, and the variety of forms they employ. Give your opinions of the poems: what do you like or dislike about them?

The tale of a glorious end

This drawing below appeared in the *Illustrated London News* of Christmas 1914. It shows war as people wanted to see it: as noble, heroic sacrifice. Discuss the details of the picture: the sword on the table; the portrait; the friend's slight wound; the old man's pose; the young wife's expression; the grey-haired mother.

Dead man on the battlefield

As preparation for his majestic war memorials, the sculptor Charles Jagger did this battlefield sketch in 1918. Contrast its horrible details with *The tale of a glorious end*.

Study for his sculpture *No man's land*: Charles Jagger

The tale of a glorious end: A.C Michael

UNIT 9 //
Realities of trench warfare

The Western Front was a maze of trenches stretching 720 kilometres across Europe from Switzerland to the Belgian coast. It was created after the failure of the Germans to defeat France quickly, as they had planned to do, by sweeping through Belgium to capture Paris. In September 1914, Britain and France held this advance at the decisive Battle of the Marne, and pushed back the Germans. As winter approached, both sides dug defensive lines of trenches. These were extended northward during the 'race to the sea' of late-1914. Both sides paused to rebuild their forces and the trenches were developed into a vast complex of ditches.

> All the spectacular side of war was gone, never to reappear... trenches and always trenches and nothing showing above the surface of the ground. Day after day the butchery of the unknown by the unseen...

The Times, 24 November 1914

Until 1918, the line seemed impossible to break. The mighty artillery ruled the battlefields. However, it was the weapons of defence, the barbed wire and the machine-gun, that held up and cut down would-be attackers and that produced the trench stalemate of 1915-18.

The ideal trench was 2 metres (6 feet) deep with sandbag parapets, fire-steps for sentries, and wooden duck-boards laid over drainage channels. Few trenches were ideal. Some seemed to be built of the men who had died defending them.

> Every square yard of ground seemed to be layered with corpses, producing a sickening stench ... A swollen right arm, with a German eagle tattooed on it, used to stick out and brush us as we squeezed by ...

George Coppard, from *With a Machine-gun to Cambrai* 1969

The power of the artillery: *War drawing no.2*: P. Wyndham Lewis

Rain, mud, rats, lice, and tiredness, fear and boredom were the daily realities of trench life. There were months of tedium. Then a raid across No Man's Land, between the trench lines, to attack the enemy, released furious violence.

> The British flung in on top of the defenders like terriers into a rat pit, and the fighters snarled and worried and scuffled and clutched and tore at each other more like savage brutes than men. The defence was not broken or driven out - it was killed out; and lunging bayonet and smashing butt caught and finished the few that tried to struggle and claw a way out of the slippery trench sides.

Boyd Cable, from *Between the Lines* 1915

The British war effort was dominated by the vast battles of the Somme (1916) and Ypres (1917), which lasted for months, involved millions of men, and absorbed thousands of lives.

The artist Paul Nash painted the hideous battlefields around Ypres and wrote an angry protest about them in a letter home.

> The rain drives on, the stinking mud becomes more evilly yellow, the shell-holes fill up with green-white water ... the black, dying trees ooze and sweat and the shells never cease ... annihilating, maiming, maddening they plunge into the grave which is this land; one huge grave and cast upon it the poor dead. It is unspeakable, godless, hopeless ...

Paul Nash, November 1917

Gilbert Frankau described the pitiless trench fighting of 1918. Like others, he admired the courage, endurance and skill of the fighting soldier.

> That figure in sodden khaki, cumbered with ugly gear, its precious rifle wrapped in rags, no brightness anywhere about it except the light of its eyes ... It broke the Hindenburg Line. Its body was thrown to fill the trenches it had won.

H.M. Tomlinson: from *Waiting for daylight* 1922

The Harvest of Battle, by C.R.W. Nevinson, shows the horrific wasteland made by endless trench warfare.

from: THE SONG OF THE RED-EDGED STEEL

Then the death-light lit our faces,
     And the death-mist floated red
O'er the crimsoned cratered places
     Where his outposts crouched in dread…
And we stabbed or clubbed them as they crouched;
     and shot them as they fled;…

So we laboured – while we lasted:
     Soaked in rain or parched in sun;
Bullet-riddled ; fire-blasted;
     Poisoned ; fodder for the gun:
So we perished, and our bodies rotted in the ground
     they won.

GILBERT FRANKAU

Much criticism has been levelled at the First World War generals for their disastrous mismanagement of the war, although some recent historians have defended them, pointing, rightly, to the Allied battle triumphs of summer 1918. However, those who were there – junior officers, journalists, soldier poets – tell another story, especially about the costly failures of 1915–17.

They saw the generals as elderly men who had grown up in the cavalry-dominated armies of the late-nineteenth century. They did not understand the new technology that had led to the stalemate of the trenches, and their dream was always to smash a hole in the line so that the cavalry could go through to restore open warfare. Meanwhile, in their bloody attempts to break the German Front, they were content, in Winston Churchill's words, 'to fight machine-gun bullets with the breasts of gallant men'. Moreover, they and their Staff officers lived in comfortable headquarters far from the Front. They understood little of local conditions as they drew up their battle plans.

The war correspondent, Philip Gibbs, wrote bitterly about the British Army Commander's Headquarters at Montreuil, which he called 'a City of Beautiful Nonsense'.

One came to GHQ from journeys over the wild desert of the battlefields, where men lived in ditches, muddy, miserable in all things but spirit, as to a place where the pageantry of war still maintained its old and dead tradition. … It was as though men were playing at war here, while others, sixty miles away, were fighting and dying, in mud and gas waves and explosive barrages …

Often one saw the Commander-in-chief starting for an afternoon ride, a fine figure, nobly mounted, with an escort of Lancers. A pretty sight, with fluttering pennons on all their lances, and horses groomed to the last hair. It was prettier than the real thing up in the Salient or beyond the Somme, where dead bodies lay in upheaved earth among ruins and slaughtered trees. … Such careless-hearted courage when British soldiers were being blown to bits, gassed, blinded, maimed and shell-shocked in places that were far – so very far – from GHQ!

Philip Gibbs, *Realities of War* 1920

Men who had to fight the nightmare battles of the Western Front felt that the picture of war as a knightly adventure was false and stupid. A new, plain, blunt style of poem showed the horrors forcefully. Old-fashioned epic language gave way to up-to-date **colloquialism** and soldiers' slang.

Arthur Graeme West joined up straight from school, full of ideals, but he soon lost his enthusiasm for the war. He came to hate the army, feeling himself as 'a creature caught in a net'. In summer 1916 (as he records in his remarkable *Diary of a dead officer*), his reading of pacifist thinkers like Bertrand Russell almost caused him to refuse further military service. However, he returned to the Front and on 3 April 1917, he was killed by a sniper.

God! How I hate you (an extract of which is over the page) was the only poem he saw published. Originally called *War poets* and aimed at Rupert Brooke and his imitators, the poem's second draft focused on Hugh Freston, a young soldier poet idealist killed in 1916. In *O fortunati* (The lucky ones), Freston claimed to be glad and proud to fight:

Oh happy to have lived these epic days!
To have seen unfold, as doth a dream unfold,
These glorious chivalries, these dreams
of gold …

West uses horrific details of trench fighting to answer him.

from: GOD! HOW I HATE YOU

God! how I hate you, you young cheerful men,
Whose pious poetry blossoms on your graves
As soon as you are in them …
                              Hark how one chants –
'Oh happy to have lived these epic days' –
'These epic days'! And *he'd* been to France,
And seen the trenches, glimpsed the huddled dead
In the periscope, hung on the rusty wire:
Choked by their sickly foetor,[1] day and night
Blown down his throat: stumbled through ruined
   hearths,
Proved all that muddy brown monotony
Where blood's the only coloured thing. Perhaps
Had seen a man killed, a sentry shot at night,
Hunched as he fell, his feet on the firing-step,
His neck against the back slope of the trench,
And the rest doubled between, his head
Smashed like an eggshell and the warm grey brain
Spattered all bloody on the parados[2] …
Yet still God's in His Heaven, all is right
In this best possible of worlds …

ARTHUR GRAEME WEST

[1] **foetor:** *stink*
[2] **parados:** *rear sandbag parapet of trench*

◉ CLOSE STUDY

1   West answers Freston's **sonnet** in two different ways. One way is his use of powerful and vivid details of misery and death in the trenches. Pick out and list several of these horrible word pictures.

2   West also uses a blunt, plain, **colloquial** tone. Select some of his **colloquialisms**.

3   Look at West's **adjectives** and **verbs**. Which do you think are most striking?

4   The last line is based on *Candide*, a novel by the eighteenth century French writer, Voltaire, whose character Pangloss is a determined optimist. He believes that ours is 'the best possible of all worlds'. Do you like this **sarcastic** ending?

Gilbert Frankau also attacked the heroic-style war poets. He had read the poems of a fellow officer who had been promoted to the Staff and so had escaped the trenches. He wrote him a verse letter, called *The Other Side*, from which these are extracts.

A landscape of corpses: Otto Dix

from: THE OTHER SIDE

My grief, but we're fed up to the back teeth
With war-books, war-verse, all the eye-wash stuff
That seems to please the idiots at home.
You know the kind of thing, or used to know:
'Heroes who laugh while Fritz is strafing them' –
(I don't remember that *you* found it fun,
The day they shelled us out of Blaauwport Farm!)
'After the fight. Our cheery wounded. Note
The smile of victory: it won't come off' –
(Of course they smile; so'd you, if you'd escaped,
And saw three months of hospital ahead …
They don't smile, much, when they're shipped
  back to France!)
But what's the good of war-books, if they fail
To give civilian-readers an idea
Of what life *is* like in the firing line. …

You might have done that much; from you, at least,
I thought we'd get an inkling of the truth.
But no; you rant and rattle, beat your drum,
And blow your two-penny trumpet like the rest:
'Red battle's glory,' 'Honour's utmost task,'
'Gay jesting faces of undaunted boys,' …
The same old Boy's-Own-Paper balderdash! …

Lord, if I'd half *your* brains, I'd write a book:
None of your sentimental platitudes,
But something real, vital; that should strip
The glamour from this outrage we call war,
Showing it naked, hideous, stupid, vile –
One vast abomination. So that they
Who, coming after, till the ransomed fields
Where our lean corpses rotted in the ooze,
Reading my written words, should understand
This stark stupendous horror, visualise
The unutterable foulness of it all. …
I'd show them, not your glamorous 'glorious game,'
Which men play 'jesting' 'for their honour's sake' –
(A kind of Military Tournament,
With just a hint of danger – bound in cloth!) –
But War, – as war is now, and always was:
A dirty, loathsome, servile murder-job:–
Men, lousy, sleepless, ulcerous, afraid,
Toiling their hearts out in the pulling slime
That wrenches gum-boot down from bleeding heel
And cakes in itching arm-pits, navel, ears:
Men stunned to brainlessness, and gibbering:
Men driving men to death, and worse than death:
Men maimed and blinded: men against machines –
Flesh versus iron, concrete, flame and wire:
Men choking out their souls in poison-gas:
Men squelched into the slime by trampling feet:
Men, disembowelled by guns five miles away,
Cursing, with their last breath, the living God
Because He made them, in His image, men. …
So – were your talent mine – I'd write of war
For those who, coming after, know it not. …

GILBERT FRANKAU

☉ CLOSE STUDY

1 Frankau uses soldiers' **slang** as part of his effect here. Find some examples. Then find some words and phrases from typical 'heroic' war poets and newspapermen.

2 How does Frankau use exact, horrible details?

3 What does he want to do to the reader?

4 What is the purpose of the long list of war's horrors at the end of the extract?

5 What is Frankau's **intention** in this poem?

✎ WRITING

Imagine that you are a young officer writing to a soldier poet friend at home, whose sentimental 'heroic' war poems you dislike. Borrow ideas and style from Frankau's poem to compose a letter describing the true nature of war and correcting your friend's ideas of it.

📖 COMPARING POEMS

Consider the two poems by West and Frankau. Compare them with *The Volunteer* by Herbert Asquith and *Peace* by Rupert Brooke (p.42). Write about the contrasting attitudes, themes, language and style.

The Battle of the Somme (July–November 1916), with its enormous losses and indecisive advances, marked the end of the heroic idealism of 1914–15.

Robert Graves, a famous poet, also produced one of the best-known First World War memoirs, *Goodbye to all that*. He fought at the Somme and was severely wounded. Mametz Wood had been turned into a formidable battlefield fortress by the Germans.

A DEAD BOCHE[1]

To you who'd read my songs of War
  And only hear of blood and fame,
I'll say (you've heard it said before)
  'War's Hell!' and if you doubt the same,
Today I found in Mametz Wood
A certain cure for lust of blood:

Where, propped against a shattered trunk,
  In a great mess of things unclean,
Sat a dead Boche; he scowled and stunk
  With clothes and face a sodden green,
Big-bellied, spectacled, crop-haired,
Dribbling black blood from nose and beard.

ROBERT GRAVES

[1] **Boche**: *German*

1 What is 'lust of blood'?

2 What is so horrible about the dead German?

3 Why is he a 'certain cure'? What is Graves' message here?

4 Do you like the **plain language** of the poem?

A.E. Tomlinson went from Cambridge University to the hell of the Somme. He wrote several forceful poems about the war but this, one of the most outspoken, was not published until 1997.

MANSLAUGHTER MORNING

On Manslaughter Morning in Massacre Wood
I see a sentry shoot his best friend's face away,
Cleaning his rifle at dawn stand-down.

They take him away with a sort of kind contempt,
A death among deathless deaths, a name among
    nameless names
Duly reported to the ginger-haired captain.

In the Battle of the Somme
I see thirty khaki citizens
Carrying sandbags full of hand-bombs
Slung over khaki shoulders.
Resting on a green bank,
One citizen drops his bag carelessly
To rest on foreign clay.

The explosion blows his back out,
The small of his back out,
The small of his back and webbing and khaki!
I see his inside
Like an operating table model,
For he is dead but not quite dead,
And his limbs ache with war!
At midnight in murder time
Along Looney Bin Lane,
The Line is lousy with loose metal!
Sandbags quake, men cower and from world's outer end
Stumbles a figure, eyeless for ever!

Helmet-less, he tries to hold his face shreds
With both blind hands!
More terrible than multitudes howling
Is his last blind silence!
From fingers pressed against blood,
Blood comes pouring down his wrist,
Drenching boots, puttees, tunic;
Still dabbling at the petalled mask, once a man's face,
And stretched on the long duckboards,
He groans his last,
Fingers clenching and unclenching
Like a pleased cat!

A.E. TOMLINSON

1 Tomlinson illustrates the chaos and horror of the Somme in three incidents. What are these?

2 What is so terrible about the line 'A death among deathless deaths, a name among nameless names'?

3 This poem's **tone** is different from the anger of West, Frankau and Graves. A **sardonic** black humour is Tomlinson's style. Find examples of this in words and sentences.

4 Grotesque **comparisons** are another feature of this poem. Find some **similes** and **metaphors** here. Which have most power?

Siegfried Sassoon (see pp.67–72) expressed the post-Somme style most strongly. In this extract from *Counter-Attack*, he describes how British troops capture a German trench system. As dawn comes, they realize the horror of their surroundings.

from: COUNTER-ATTACK

We'd gained our first objective hours before
While dawn broke like a face with blinking eyes,
Pallid, unshaved and thirsty, blind with smoke,
Things seemed all right at first. We held their line,
With bombers posted, Lewis guns well placed,
And clink of shovels deepening the shallow trench.

The place was rotten with dead; green clumsy legs
High-booted, sprawled and grovelled along the saps
And trunks, face downward, in the sucking mud,
Wallowed like trodden sand-bags loosely filled;
And naked sodden buttocks, mats of hair,
Bulged, clotted heads slept in the plastering slime.
And then the rain began, – the jolly old rain!

SIEGFRIED SASSOON

1 What is the dawn compared to and why is this especially suitable?

2 What do the men discover as daylight comes?

3 Sassoon uses words that are not only about ugly ideas but are also ugly to say. Pick out some of these.

4 What is Sassoon's **intention** in this extract?

Although English-born, Robert Service had made his name with verses about the American West. A Red Cross stretcher-bearer at the Front in France, he wrote many strongly felt – and now unjustly neglected – poems about what he saw. *On the wire* records a wretched, slow death: a wounded man, who cannot be rescued, is trapped in barbed wire in No Man's Land.

Barbed wire: Louis Raemaekers

from: ON THE WIRE

O God, take the sun from the sky!
It's burning me, scorching me up.
God, can't You hear my cry?
Water! A poor, little cup!
It's laughing, the cursed sun!
See how it swells and swells
Fierce as a hundred hells!
God, will it never have done?
It's searing the flesh on my bones;
It's beating with hammers red
My eyeballs into my head;
It's parching my very moans.
See! It's the size of the sky,
And the sky is a torrent of fire,
Foaming on me as I lie
Here on the wire … the wire …

Of the thousands that wheeze and hum
Heedlessly over my head,
Why can't a bullet come,
Pierce to my brain instead,
Blacken forever my brain?
Finish forever my pain?
Here in the hellish glare
Why must I suffer so?
Is it God doesn't care?
Is it God doesn't know?
Oh, to be killed outright,
Clean in the clash of the fight!
That is a golden death,
That is a boon; but this …
Drawing an anguished breath
Under a hot abyss,
Under a stooping sky
Of seething, sulphurous fire,
Scorching me up as I lie
Here on the wire … the wire …

ROBERT SERVICE

🔍 CLOSE STUDY

1   The sun is a torment to the trapped man. Which **participles** express its fierce power?

2   Comment on the choice of **comparisons** used for the sun and for the sky.

3   Usually bullets are to be feared. Why would one be a blessing here?

4   How would the soldier *like* to die?

5   How does he feel about God?

6   How is the story of Christ's crucifixion echoed here?

7   Why repeat 'the wire' twice?

Schoolmaster and poet, Cameron Wilson volunteered in 1914 and rose rapidly through the ranks. He was killed in March 1918. In his fine letters, he saw the war as 'indescribably disgusting ... a great dirty tragedy.' But for him, the hideous trench world was lit up by soldiers' comradeship and courage.

from: FRANCE 1917

... The bodies of men lay down in the dark of the earth:
Young flesh, through which life shines a friendly flame,
Was crumbled green in the fingers of decay. ...
Among the last year's oats and thistles lay
A forgotten boy, who hid as though in shame
A face that the rats had eaten. ... Thistle seeds
Danced daintily above the rebel weeds.

Old wire[1] crept through the grass there like a snake,
Orange-red in the sunlight, cruel as lust.
And a dead hand groped up blindly from the mould ...
A dandelion flamed through ribs[2] – like a heart of gold,
And a stink of rotten flesh came up from the dust ...
With a twinkle of little wings against the sun
A lark praised God for all that he had done.

There was nothing here that moved but a lonely bird,
And the wind over the grass. Men lived in mud;
Slept as their dead must sleep, walled in with clay,
Yet staring out across the unpitying day,
Staring hard-eyed like hawks that hope for blood.
The still land was a witch who held her breath,
And with a lidless eye kept watch for death.

I found honour here at last on the Earth, where man faced man;
It reached up like a lily from the filth and flies,
It grew from war as a lily from manure.
Out of the dark it burst – undaunted, sure,
As the crocus, insolent under slaty skies,
Strikes a green sword-blade through the stubborn mould,
And throws in the teeth of Winter its challenge of gold.

T.P. CAMERON WILSON

---

[1] **wire:** *barbed wire*
[2] **ribs:** *soldier's skeleton*

CLOSE STUDY

1 What is so pitiful about the dead in stanza 1?

2 What are the **ironies** of the second stanza?

3 What are the features of the trench landscape?

4 To what is the 'still land' **compared** in stanza 3?

5 What consolation does Wilson find in stanza 4 and how does his choice of **language** help you to understand its significance?

6 'Honour' was a vague idea in 1914. Now it seems very real. What is contained in the idea here?

7 How does the last stanza relate to these other lines from the poem?

On every road War spilled her hurried men,
And I saw their courage, young and eagle strong
Great love I saw, though these men feared the name
And hid their greatness as a kind of shame ...

WRITING

1 Look back over the poems and extracts in this section. Drawing on your reading and making reference to the texts, write a discursive essay on the theme of either 'The trench landscape' or 'Men at the Front'. You should aim to be informative while providing an analysis of how different writers have portrayed the subject.

2 Read over the poems in this section, and study the powerful paintings, drawings and photographs included here. Make notes on details that impress you. Then try writing your own angry, graphic war poem about the horrors of the Western Front, and the courage and endurance of the soldiers there.

3 Choose two poems from this section. Discuss how they use

• realistic pictures of trench incidents
• horrible details
• plain **colloquial** language
• forceful **imagery**

COMPARING POEMS

Choose two of the poems from 'Ideals and chivalry' (pp. 42-46) and two from 'Realities of trench warfare'. Compare and contrast their

• attitudes to men in battle
• vague abstraction / forceful realism
• language and imagery

UNIT 10 //

Comrades: A verse short story

Robert Nichols served briefly with the Royal Artillery before being invalided home with 'shell shock'. His poems caused much interest because of their surprise effects and realism. He enjoyed brief fame and gave poetry readings at home and in the USA.

Comrades: An Episode is a story about the close relationship between an officer and his men. When Gates, the officer, is hit and badly wounded, he manages to crawl back across No Man's Land to his own parapet, the raised line of sandbangs along the front of the trench. There two of his own men sacrifice their lives trying to save him.

In a world where life seemed pointless and death always near, only comradeship remained as a worthwhile purpose. An article in the *Nation* magazine noted that 'the great spiritual bond in the army is that of comradeship'. An officer, Roland Feilding, wrote to his wife in 1916:

In spite of the gloominess of the surroundings, there was an atmosphere of selflessness the like of which has probably not been seen in the world before ... Such is the influence of the shells.

War letters to a wife: 1929

British soldiers on the Somme, July 1916

COMRADES: AN EPISODE

Before, before he was aware
The 'Verey' light[1] had risen … on the air
It hung glistering …
          And he could not stay his hand
From moving to the barbed wire's broken strand.
A rifle cracked.
          He fell.
Night waned. He was alone. A heavy shell
Whispered itself passing high, high overhead.
His wound was wet to his hand: for still it bled
On to the glimmering ground.
Then with a slow, vain smile his wound he bound,
Knowing, of course, he'd not see home again –
Home whose thought he put away.
          His men
Whispered: 'Where's Mister Gates?' 'Out on the
wire.'
'I'll get him,' said one …
          Dawn blinked, and the fire
Of the Germans heaved up and down the line.
'Stand to!'[2]
          Too late! 'I'll get him.' 'O the swine!
When we might get him in yet safe and whole!'
'Corporal didn't see 'un fall out on patrol.
Or he'd 'a got 'un.' 'Sssh!'
          'No talking there.'
A whisper: ' 'A went down at the last flare.'
Meanwhile the Maxims[3] toc-toc-tocked; their swish
Of bullets told death lurked against the wish.
No hope for him!
          His corporal, as one shamed,
Vainly and helplessly his ill-luck blamed.

*   *   *   *   *

Then Gates slowly saw the morn
Break in a rosy peace through the lone thorn
By which he lay, and felt the dawn-wind pass
Whispering through the pallid, stalky grass
Of No-Man's Land …
          And the tears came
Scaldingly sweet, more lovely than a flame.
He closed his eyes: he thought of home
And grit his teeth. He knew no help could come …

*   *   *   *   *

The silent sun over the earth held sway,
Occasional rifles cracked and far away
A heedless speck, a 'plane, slid on alone,
Like a fly traversing a cliff of stone.

'I must get back', said Gates aloud, and heaved
At his body. But it lay bereaved
Of any power. He could not wait till night …
And he lay still. Blood swam across his sight.
Then with a groan:
'No luck ever! Well, I must die alone'.

Occasional rifles cracked. A cloud that shone,
Gold-rimmed, blackened the sun and then was
        gone …
The sun still smiled. The grass sang in its play.
Someone whistled: 'Over the hills and far away'.
Gates watched silently the swift, swift sun
Burning his life before it was begun …

Suddenly he heard Corporal Timmins' voice: 'Now
    then,
'Urry up with that tea.'
          'Hi Ginger!' 'Bill!' His men!
Timmins and Jones and Wilkinson (the 'bard'),
And Hughes and Simpson. It was hard
Not to see them: Wilkinson, stubby, grim,
With his 'No, sir', 'Yes, sir,' and the slim
Simpson: 'Indeed, sir?' (while it seemed he winked
Because his smiling left eye always blinked)
And Corporal Timmins, straight and blond and wise,
With his quiet-scanning, level, hazel eyes;
And all the others … tunics that didn't fit …
A dozen different sorts of eyes. O it
Was hard to lie there! Yet he must. But no:
'I've got to die. I'll get to them. I'll go'.

Inch by inch he fought, breathless and mute,
Dragging his carcase like a famished brute …
His head was hammering, and his eyes were dim;
A bloody sweat seemed to ooze out of him
And freeze along his spine … Then he'd lie still
Before another effort of his will
Took him one nearer yard.

*   *   *   *   *

          The parapet was reached.
He could not rise to it. A lookout screeched:
'Mr Gates!'
          Three figures in one breath
Leaped up. Two figures fell in toppling death;
And Gates was lifted in. 'Who's hit?' said he.
'Timmins and Jones.' 'Why did they that for me? –
I'm gone already!' Gently they laid him prone
And silently watched.
          He twitched. They heard him moan
'Why for me?' His eyes roamed round, and none
    replied.
'I see it was alone I should have died.'
They shook their heads. Then, 'Is the doctor here?'
'He's coming, sir; he's hurryin', no fear.'
'No good …
          Lift me.' They lifted him.
He smiled and held his arms out to the dim,
And in a moment passed beyond their ken,
Hearing him whisper, 'O my men, my men!'

ROBERT NICHOLS

---

[1] **Verey light:** *flare to light up trench area*
[2] **Stand to:** *trench alert at dawn*
[3] **Maxims:** *machine-guns*

CLOSE STUDY

Section 1: 'Before, before … he put away'

The young officer, 'Mr Gates', has gone out at night, with his corporal, Timmins, into No Man's land to cut the German barbed-wire before a raid.

1   What exactly happens to Gates?

2   Why use so many **short sentences** here?

3   When he is conscious again, what does Gates think of and then try *not* to think of?

Section 2: 'His men … his ill luck blamed'

The corporal has returned to his own lines. He guesses bitterly that Gates was left by the enemy wire. 'Stand to' comes at dawn. Firing was often heavy at that time.

4   Why was it so difficult for the men in Gates' company to go out into No Man's Land to rescue their officer?

5   How does Nichols use snippets of dialogue here?

Section 3: 'Then Gates … before it was begun'

Gates lies out in No Man's Land and Nichols cleverly conveys the atmosphere so the reader can clearly picture the scene.

6   What does Gates see and hear around him as time passes?

7   This tragic scene has been made beautiful by Nichols' use of language. Select and comment on some examples.

Section 4: 'Suddenly he heard … "I'll go".'

Gates hears the voices of his men talking in the front line.

8   How does Nichols suggest Gates' affection for his men?

Section 5: 'Inch by inch … "my men!"'

Gates crawls painfully back to his own trench position but he cannot climb over the parapet.

9   What exactly happens at the end?

10   What are Gates' last thoughts?

11   What does the conclusion show about men in battle?

WRITING

Imagine that one of Gates' men, Wilkinson, writes a letter home to his brother. Write the letter, describing the events of *Comrades*. Start with the night patrol going out, and end with Gates' last words. You will need to add some material from your own imagination.

'Stand to' before dawn: John Nash

UNIT 11 // Spring offensive

Each year of the First World War was marked by massive spring attacks by one side or the other. All were unsuccessful until the Germans finally smashed the Western Front in March 1918. Many writers noted the contrast between the new life and energy of spring, and the death and destruction of battle.

A little group of men with scarlet staff-bands on their caps and tabs on their collars climb out of the cars and prod sticks at the ground, stamp on it, dig a heel in, to test its hardness and dryness ... To these men the 'Promise of Spring' is the promise of the crescendo of battle and slaughter.

The General and his staff are standing in the middle of a wide patch of poppies, spread out in a bright scarlet that matches exactly the red splashes on the brows and throats of the group. They move slowly back towards the cars, and as they walk the red ripples and swirls against their boots and about their knees.

One might imagine them wading knee deep in a river of blood ...

Boyd Cable, from *Between the Lines* 1916

Wilfred Owen's last poem is based on this contrast. He had taken part in an attack in May 1917, which he described in a letter.

The sensations of going over the top are about as exhilarating as those dreams of falling over a precipice. ... There was an extraordinary exultation in the act of slowly walking forward, showing ourselves openly. ... When I looked back and saw the ground all crawling and wormy with wounded bodies, I felt no horror at all but only an immense exultation at having got through the barrage ...

Wilfred Owen, 17 May 1917

He used some of these ideas in the poem. Soldiers (probably British, but no nationality is specified, as in most of Owen's 1918 poems) are resting before beginning an attack on a hill in front of them, on the far side of which their enemies are dug into trenches. It is May and the French countryside they have passed through looks beautiful.

SPRING OFFENSIVE

Halted against the shade of a last hill
They fed, and eased of pack-loads, were at ease;
And leaning on the nearest chest or knees
Carelessly slept.
          But many there stood still
To face the stark blank sky beyond the ridge,
Knowing their feet had come to the end of the world.
Marvelling they stood, and watched the long grass swirled
By the May breeze, murmurous with wasp and midge;
And though the summer oozed into their veins
Like an injected drug for their bodies' pains,
Sharp on their souls hung the imminent ridge of grass,
Fearfully flashed the sky's mysterious glass.

Hour after hour they ponder[1] the warm field
And the far valley behind, where buttercups
Had blessed with gold their slow boots coming up;
When even the little brambles would not yield
But clutched and clung to them like sorrowing arms.
They breathe like trees unstirred.

Till like a cold gust thrills the little word
At which each body and its soul begird[2]
And tighten them for battle. No alarms
Of bugles, no high flags, no clamorous haste, –
Only a lift and flare of eyes that faced
The sun, like a friend with whom their love is done.
O larger shone that smile against the sun, –
Mightier than his whose bounty these have spurned.

So, soon they topped the hill, and raced together
Over an open stretch of herb and heather
Exposed. And instantly the whole sky burned
With fury against them; earth set sudden cups
In thousands for their blood; and the green slope
Chasmed and deepened sheer to infinite space.

Of them who running on that last high place
Breasted the surf of bullets, or went up
On the hot blast and fury of hell's upsurge,
Or plunged and fell away past this world's verge,
Some say God caught them even before they fell.

But what say such as from existence' brink
Ventured but drave[3] too swift to sink,
The few who rushed in the body to enter hell,
And there out-fiending all its fiends and flames
With superhuman inhumanities,
Long-famous glories, immemorial shames –
And crawling slowly back, have by degrees
Regained cool peaceful air in wonder –
Why speak not they of comrades that went under?

WILFRED OWEN

[1] **ponder:** *think about*
[2] **begird:** *get ready*
[3] **drave:** *drove*

CLOSE STUDY

Section 1: 'Halted against ... like trees unstirred'

1 The soldiers rest before the attack on the hill. Some sleep, using each other's bodies as pillows. The more imaginative look at the landscape. When they look in front of them, what two threatening things do they see?

2 What do they lovingly watch behind them?

3 Why is the 'warm field' so impressive?

4 Why do they ponder (think about) it?

Section 2: 'Till like a cold gust .. before they fell'

5 What is the dramatic 'little word'?

6 What do they do as they prepare for battle?

7 They say goodbye – to what?
Why is this significant?

8 What commences when the enemy sees them and what happens to some men on 'the green slope'?

Section 3: 'But what say such ... that went under'

The last section concentrates on the survivors, who have been on the edge of life ('existence' brink'). They did terrible things in the fighting ('superhuman inhumanities') but somehow survived. They return to the place where they rested before battle and enjoy 'cool peaceful air'.

9 Whom, surprisingly, do they not talk about?

10 What do they relish about being alive?

11 Look again at section 1. Owen imitates his favourite poet, John Keats, in evoking the heat and sleepiness of a May day in the countryside. He copies the **onomatopoeic** 's' and 'z' sounds of Keats' *To Autumn*.

Find the lines, and the words, where Owen uses this language powerfully.

12 Look at the 'buttercups' and 'little brambles'. **Pathetic fallacy** is the projection of human feelings onto the non-human world around us. What do the buttercups and brambles seem to want to do to the men?

13 Owen's poem is rich in **imagery** and **descriptive language**. Select and comment on five examples that you like.

'Breasting the surf of bellets'. *Over the top*: Alfred Bastien

Imagine that you are one of the soldiers who survived. Keeping close to the ideas of the poem, describe your thoughts and observations before, during and after the battle in the form of a short descriptive sketch. Use language, sensory details, a variety of sentence structures and the opening and conclusion of your piece to engage the interest of the reader.

Julian Grenfell's *Into Battle* was, in its time, one of the most popular poems produced by the war. It was published in *The Times* in May 1915, shortly after Grenfell died from wounds. Whatever his private thoughts, in his letters home he put on an appearance of enjoying the fighting. 'I adore war. … It is like a big picnic. … It's all the best fun one ever dreamed of.' *Into Battle* is written in this spirit. Grenfell's picture of the soldier in spring contrasts strongly with Owen's.

Into Battle supports the glory of war as a creative force in life on earth. Charles Darwin, the nineteenth century naturalist, saw life as a struggle for survival, won by the superior species. Grenfell saw war in the same way. The soldier is an expression of the energy and strength of nature, and reflects the power and growth of the spring around him as he approaches the battlefield.

INTO BATTLE

The naked earth is warm with spring,
   And with green grass and bursting trees
Leans to the sun's gaze glorying,
   And quivers in the sunny breeze;

And life is colour and warmth and light,
   And a striving evermore for these;
And he is dead who will not fight;
   And who dies fighting has increase.

The fighting man shall from the sun
   Take warmth, and life from the glowing earth;
Speed with the light-foot winds to run,
   And with the trees to newer birth;
And find, when fighting shall be done,
   Great rest, and fullness after dearth[1].

All the bright company of Heaven
   Hold him in their high comradeship,
The Dog-Star, and the Sisters Seven,
   Orion's Belt and sworded hip.

The woodland trees that stand together,
   They stand to him each one a friend;
They gently speak in the windy weather:
   They guide to valley and ridge's end.

The kestrel hovering by day,
   And the little owls that call by night,
Bid him be swift and keen as they,
   As keen of ear, as swift of sight.

The blackbird sings to him, 'Brother, brother,
   If this be the last song you shall sing,
Sing well, for you may not sing another;
   Brother, sing.'

In dreary, doubtful, waiting hours,
   Before the brazen frenzy starts,
The horses show him nobler powers;
   O patient eyes, courageous hearts!

And when the burning moment breaks,
   And all things else are out of mind,
And only joy of battle takes
   Him by the throat, and makes him blind,

Through joy and blindness he shall know,
   Not caring much to know, that still
Nor lead nor steel shall reach him, so
   That it be not the Destined Will.

The thundering line of battle stands,
   And in the air Death moans and sings;
But Day shall clasp him with strong hands,
   And Night shall fold him in soft wings.

JULIAN GRENFELL

---

[1] **dearth:** *an inadequate amount*

CLOSE STUDY

Stanzas 1 and 2

1 Which words show the power and energy of spring?

2 What does Grenfell say about war and soldiers in lines 7 and 8?

Stanzas 3 to 8

3 In the soldier's surroundings, what various aspects of nature, and living creatures, seem to support his battle activity?

4 What qualities can he learn from each of these?

5 What is the blackbird's message?

Stanzas 9 to 11

These describe the battle itself.

6 Which key words and phrases show the fighting as glorious and exciting?

7 How does Grenfell deal with fear of death in these lines?

8 This is a poem full of bold words and ideas. It is good to recite. Which lines are most impressive?

COMPARING POEMS

Compare *Into Battle* with *Spring Offensive*.

How do the poets use spring as a background to war and battle?

How do they feel about nature and fighting?

What are their attitudes to death in war?

Compare the

- imagery
- pathetic fallacy
- diction
- style

Which is more interesting and why?

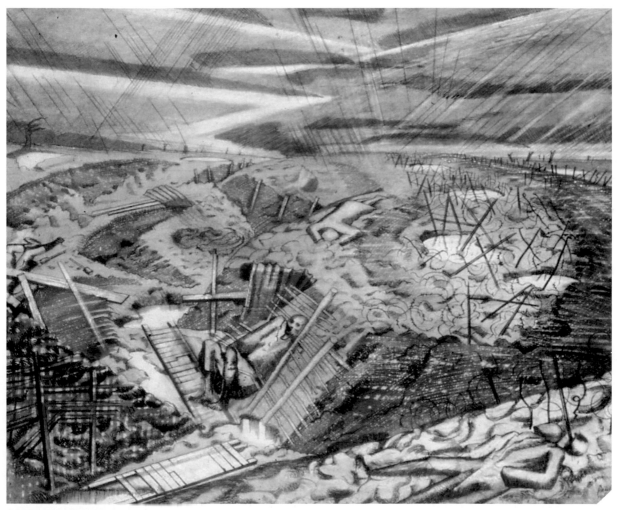

After the Battle: Paul Nash

'Winter is not the least of the horrors of war,' wrote the soldier poet Isaac Rosenberg in a letter. As a private he had to endure the hardships of the Western Front for months on end. The old idea of armies ceasing fire in autumn to retire into winter quarters had vanished by 1914. Trench fighting continued throughout the winters of the First World War. Even the famous Christmas truces, when enemies mingled cheerfully in No Man's Land, ended after 1915.

Wilfred Owen first went to the front in the Somme sector in the bitter winter of 1916-17. In February, he wrote to his mother, describing the bleak landscape of 'No-Man's Land under snow':

> My platoon had no dug-outs, but had to lie in the snow under the deadly wind... We were marooned on a frozen desert. There is not a sign of life on the horizon and a thousand signs of death. Not a blade of grass, not an insect; once or twice a day the shadow of a big hawk, scenting carrion...

Owen, who spared his mother nothing, went on to describe the frozen corpses:

> The dead, whose unburiable bodies sit outside the dug-outs all day, all night, the most execrable sights on earth...to sit with them all day, all night...and a week later to come back and find them still sitting there, in motionless groups...

Letter: 4 February 1917

He used these experiences in 'Exposure' written in early 1918. There is no fighting in the poem and 'nothing happens'. We are given the men's thoughts as they endure 'the merciless iced east winds', worse enemies than the Germans.

● CLOSE STUDY

1   The men are on guard on a winter night in a salient, where the British trench lines bulge forward into enemy territory. What do they see and hear around them? (First four stanzas)

2   The men are so dazed with cold that they fall into day-dreams. Of what two places do they fondly dream? How do the dreams end? Why is this sad? (Stanzas 5 and 6)

EXPOSURE

Our brains ache, in the merciless iced east winds that knive
    us . . .
Wearied we keep awake because the night is silent . . .
Low drooping flares confuse our memory of the salient[1] . . .
Worried by silence, sentries whisper, curious, nervous,
            But nothing happens.

Watching, we hear the mad gusts tugging on the wire.
Like twitching agonies of men among its brambles.
Northward, incessantly, the flickering gunnery rumbles,
Far off, like a dull rumour of some other war.
            What are we doing here?

The poignant misery of dawn begins to grow . . .
We only know war lasts, rain soaks, and clouds sag stormy.
Dawn massing in the east her melancholy army
Attacks once more in ranks on shivering ranks of grey,
            But nothing happens.

Sudden successive flights of bullets streak the silence.
Less deathly than the air that shudders black with snow,
With sidelong flowing flakes that flock, pause and renew,
We watch them wandering up and down the wind's
    nonchalance,
            But nothing happens.

Pale flakes with fingering stealth come feeling for our faces –
We cringe in holes, back on forgotten dreams, and stare,
    snow-dazed,
Deep into grassier ditches. So we drowse, sun-dozed,
Littered with blossoms trickling where the blackbird fusses.
    – Is it that we are dying?

Slowly our ghosts drag home: glimpsing the sunk fires, glozed[2]
With crusted dark-red jewels; crickets jingle there;
For hours the innocent mice rejoice: the house is theirs;
Shutters and doors all closed: on us the doors are closed, –
            We turn back to our dying.

Since we believe not otherwise can kind fires burn;
Nor ever suns smile true on child, or field, or fruit.
For God's invincible spring our love is made afraid;
Therefore, not loath, we lie out here; therefore were born,
            For love of God seems dying.

To-night, this frost will fasten on this mud and us,
Shrivelling many hands, puckering foreheads crisp.
The burying-party, picks and shovels in their shaking grasp,
Pause over half-known faces. All their eyes are ice,
            But nothing happens.

WILFRED OWEN

---

[1] **salient:** *where the front line juts into enemy territory*
[2] **glozed:** *an invented word, mixing glowing and glazed*

3   In their misery they console themselves with thinking that they are defending their homeland and way of life against a destructive enemy. On which particular aspects of home do they reflect? (Stanza 7)

4   The powerful conclusion shows the effects of bitter cold on living and dead. Why is the job of the burying party so difficult? Explain 'half-known faces' and 'All their eyes are ice'. (Stanza 8)

5   Look at the **imagery** of the poem. Consider these **similes** and **metaphors**:

   • *east winds that knive us*
   • *Dawn massing in the east her melancholy army*
   • *Pale flakes with fingering stealth*

   Find some other examples yourself. Then work out exactly what is compared to what in these images. Why are they appropriate and which do you find most effective?

6   Look at the **line-endings** in the poem. They are not exact rhymes based on changes in **consonant** sounds (cat / bat). They are **half-rhymes** or **para-rhymes** which were Owen's remarkable innovation (new idea) in poetry. They are based on changes in **vowel** sounds (dazed / dozed). They give the poem a tight shape without the bounce of ordinary rhyme which would be out of place in a reflective mood study like *Exposure*.

   Owen's brilliant ear for music and for the sounds of words allowed him to use the device with great power.

   Make a plan of the half-rhymes. In stanza 1, for example, the pattern is

knive us / nervous
silent / salient

Which of the pairs in your plan are impressive and which less successful?

7   **Alliteration** is the close repetition of consonant sounds at the beginning of words. Owen uses this sometimes to add emphasis to the idea in a line:

   *Pale **flakes** with **fingering** stealth come **feeling for** our **faces***

   Find other examples in the poem and list them.

8   Owen use short **chorus lines** to end stanzas. What do these add to the meaning and effect of the poem?

✏ WRITING

1   Imagine that you are one of the soldiers. Describe what you see and hear around you as you stand in the icy wind on sentry duty. Mention your day-dreams and include your reasons for enduring this difficult war service. End as you watch the burial party at work. Start your piece like this:

How do we stand it in this frozen wasteland? This is not sentry duty. It is torture! All we can hear in the black silent night are the other sentries' whispers and the wild, biting east wind in the barbed wire...

A Bombing Post in the Snow: John Nash

2 Write about *Exposure*. Consider:

- What scenes does it describe for us?

- What are the various thoughts of the men as they lie in the snow?

- What do you find interesting about Owen's **diction** and **imagery**?

- Do you like the **half-rhymes** and the short lines at the end of each stanza?

- How does the poem differ from the usual pictures of war?

- Which parts of the poem impress you most?

3 Look at the painting on the previous page by John Nash, who fought in France and Flanders. Write about the picture, describing the thoughts of one of the soldiers in the shell-hole. Use details from the picture but also include ideas from Owen's *Exposure*.

Edgell Rickword joined the army straight from school and lost an eye in fighting on the Western Front. He wrote a few poems after 1918, including this one looking back on the war.

WINTER WARFARE

Colonel Cold strode up the Line
   (tabs[1] of rime[2] and spurs of ice);
stiffened all that met his glare:
   horses, men, and lice.

Visited a forward post,
   left them burning, ear to foot;
fingers stuck to biting steel,
   toes to frozen boot.

Stalked on into No Man's Land,
   turned the wire to fleecy wool,
iron stakes to sugar sticks
   snapping at a pull.

Those who watched with hoary[3] eyes
   saw two figures gleaming there;
Hauptman Kälte, Colonel Cold,
   gaunt in the grey air.

Stiffly, tinkling spurs they moved
   glassy eyed, with glinting heel
stabbing those who lingered there
   torn by screaming steel.

EDGELL RICKWORD

[1] **tabs:** *rank flashes on collar*
[2] **rime:** *frost*
[3] **hoary:** *frosty*

1 The harsh winter is **personified** as a fierce army Colonel. Why is this appropriate?

2 In the first three stanzas, which words link 'Cold' and a senior officer?

3 Note down everything that happens to men visited by Colonel Cold.

4 In the last two stanzas, a German-named figure, Hauptman Kälte (Captain Cold), appears. What is the point of this?

5 Why do Cold and Kälte work together?

6 Rickword uses grim jokes. What are these?

7 The last two lines are particularly savage. What is happening exactly? What sad idea is expressed in the word 'linger'?

8 Where are the **rhymes** in the four line stanzas most effective?

■ COMPARING POEMS

Write about the two poems together.

Compare

- the scenes they describe
- the thoughts of the men in the trenches
- the way that the horrors of war and winter are related
- the poets' choice of words and comparisons
- the use of rhymes or varied line lengths

Which poem do you like better?

UNIT 13 //

Disabled: A victim of war

Wilfred Owen (see pp.58, 62) wrote *Disabled* while he was recovering from 'shell shock' at Craiglockhart Hospital in Edinburgh.

It was one of the first of his war poems to impress his soldier-poet friends, like Sassoon, and Robert Graves, who wrote to him:

> *Do you know, Owen, that's a damn fine poem of yours ... Really damn fine! ... Owen, you have seen things, you are a poet.*

The poem is like the photographs of badly wounded men that Owen supposedly carried with him: it wants to shock complacent civilians who support the war. The central figure is a teenager, who has volunteered under age, attracted by the glamour of army uniform. He has been so badly wounded that he has lost all his limbs. He may be imagined, or possibly a real figure that Owen has seen in Edinburgh. The poet had the power to get into the minds of other people, as he told his mother in a letter:

> *At present I am a sick man in hospital by night ... I am whatever and whoever I see while going down to Edinburgh on the tram: greengrocer, policeman, shopping lady, errand boy, paper boy, blind man, crippled Tommy ...*

Letter: 8 August 1917

Owen contrasts the young man's life now, as a limbless wreck in a wheelchair, with his previous life as a handsome sportsman admired by everyone.

DISABLED

He sat in a wheeled chair, waiting for dark,
And shivered in his ghastly suit of grey,
Legless, sewn short at elbow. Through the park
Voices of boys rang saddening like a hymn,
Voices of play and pleasure after day,
Till gathering sleep had mothered them from him.

*　　　*　　　*

About this time Town used to swing so gay
When glow-lamps budded in the light blue trees,
And girls glanced lovelier as the air grew dim, –
In the old times, before he threw away his knees.
Now he will never feel again how slim
Girls' waists are, or how warm their subtle hands;
All of them touch him like some queer disease.

*　　　*　　　*

There was an artist silly for his face,
For it was younger than his youth, last year.
Now, he is old; his back will never brace;
He's lost his colour very far from here,
Poured it down shell-holes till the veins ran dry,
And half his lifetime lapsed in the hot race
And leap of purple spurted from his thigh.

*　　　*　　　*

One time he liked a blood-smear down his leg,
After the matches, carried shoulder-high.
It was after football, when he'd drunk a peg,
He thought he'd better join. – He wonders why.
Someone had said he'd look a god in kilts,
That's why; and maybe, too, to please his Meg;
Aye, that was it, to please the giddy jilts[1]
He asked to join. He didn't have to beg;
Smiling they wrote his lie; aged nineteen years.
Germans he scarcely thought of; all their guilt,
And Austria's, did not move him. And no fears
Of Fear came yet. He thought of jewelled hilts
For daggers in plaid socks; of smart salutes;
And care of arms; and leave; and pay arrears;
Esprit de corps;[2] and hints for young recruits.
And soon, he was drafted out with drums and cheers.

*　　　*　　　*

Some cheered him home, but not as crowds cheer Goal.
Only a solemn man who brought him fruits
Thanked him; and then inquired about his soul.

*　　　*　　　*

Now, he will spend a few sick years in institutes,
And do what things the rules consider wise,
And take whatever pity they may dole.
To-night he noticed how the women's eyes
Passed from him to the strong men that were whole.
How cold and late it is! Why don't they come
And put him into bed? Why don't they come?

WILFRED OWEN

[1] **jilts:** *girls*
[2] **esprit de corps:** *soldierly spirit*

CLOSE STUDY

Sections 1-3

1   Create a two-column table, contrasting on one side the man's previous life and experience, with his present experience in the right hand column.

2   What effect is created by Owen **juxtaposing** the man's past with his present like this? Comment on one of the contrasts to support your answer.

Section 4

This is a longer flashback to a year earlier.

3   Why did his friends admire him then?

4   What various reasons made him join up under age?

5   What two things did he not understand about war?

Section 5

6   How exactly did his return home, wounded, contrast with his departure?

7   Why are the 'cheers' different from those of his sporting success?

8   Who now cares about him?

Section 6

9   What is his future?

10   How do women treat him now?

11   Why does he long to escape into sleep?

DISCUSSION

1   Owen sees the soldier as the victim of various influences on him. Discuss some of these that are mentioned in the poem:

- the attraction of military uniform
- cheering crowds
- sport
- women
- alcohol
- the recruiting sergeant

2   Owen is known for his sensory **style**, where he makes us share experience through our senses of sight, touch and hearing. Find and discuss examples of this in the poem.

WRITING

1   Write a story about this young battle victim. Start with his life before the war, explain how he joined up and what happened to him, and end with him as the lonely figure in the park. Include Owen's angry feelings about the way that the young man has been treated.

---

2   How does Owen illustrate his favourite theme, 'the pity of war', in this story of the mutilated young soldier? Consider:

- The poem's focus on one individual
- The contrasts between the man's previous life and his present life
- The man's reasons for joining the army
- The man's future
- Owen's use of language.

3   Imagine that Meg visits him in hospital. What do they say to each other (bring in pre-war memories)? What are their thoughts about each other? Will Meg keep up the relationship or abandon her friend?

Compose the story from her point of view. Use plenty of detail from the poem.

4   Look at this picture of wounded men in Brighton in 1916: the hospital there specialized in limb amputations. Imagine the thoughts of the girl, and the mother, about the men. What are the men's thoughts

- about the child
- their war service
- their previous lives?

Wounded British soldiers on Brighton sea-front, 1916: William Hatherell

UNIT 14 //
Sassoon's rebellion

Siegfried Sassoon was a gallant officer, who won the Military Cross for courage and fought at several battles, yet he also detested the slaughter and the misconduct of the war by generals and politicians. His protest took two forms: his celebrated statement against the war, which was published in *The Times*, and his deadly, satirical war poems, which he called 'trench rockets sent up to illuminate the gloom'. Winston Churchill called them 'cries of pain wrung from soldiers during a test to destruction'.

Sassoon came from a wealthy banking family. After studying at Cambridge, he was able to live without a profession and devoted himself to hunting, riding and cricket, and to poetry, which he published at his own expense.

When war came, he quickly volunteered and became an officer in the Royal Welch Fusiliers. His war diary recorded his experiences of the Front.

> If you search carefully, you may find a skull, eyeless, grotesquely matted with what was once hair; eyes once looked from these detestable holes ... they were lit with triumph and beautiful with pity ...

30 March 1916

In July 1916, he took part in the murderous opening of the Battle of the Somme.

> The dead are terrible and undignified carcasses, stiff and contorted ... some side by side on their backs with bloody clotted fingers mingled as if they were hand-shaking in the companionship of death. And the stench undefinable. And rags and shreds of blood-stained cloth, bloody boots riddled and torn ...

14 July 1916

On leave after illness, he began his first anti-war poems, later published in *The Old Huntsman* (1917). In 1917, he returned to France and fought in the Battle of Arras.

> Two mud-stained hands were sticking out of the wet, ashen, chalky soil, like the roots of a shrub turned upside down. They might have been imploring; they might have been groping and struggling for life and release; but the dead man was hidden; he was buried ...

19 April 1917

Siegfried Sassoon, painted in summer 1917, at the time of his protest against the war: Glyn Philpot

Sassoon was wounded and sent home. In a London hospital, he was haunted by hideous dreams about the war.

> When the lights are out, and the ward is half shadow ... then the horrors come creeping across the floor; the floor is littered with parcels of dead flesh and bones, faces glaring at the ceiling ... hands clutching neck or belly ...

23 April 1917

In June 1917, he began his personal crusade against the fighting, influenced both by his own experiences and by the writing of Pacifists such as Bertrand Russell. Refusing military duties, he sent a protest statement to his commanding officer and to the press. This is an extract:

> I am making this statement as an act of wilful defiance of military authority, because I believe that the War is being deliberately prolonged by those who have the power to end it. I am a soldier, convinced that I am acting on behalf of soldiers. I believe that this War, upon which I entered as a war of defence and liberation, has now become a war of aggression and conquest ...
>
> I have seen and endured the sufferings of the troops, and I can no longer be a party to prolonging those sufferings for ends which I believe to be evil and unjust ...

In Liverpool, while Sassoon's case was being discussed, he tore the Military Cross ribbon from his tunic and threw it into the River Mersey. He was declared shell-shocked and was sent to Craiglockhart Hospital in Edinburgh. There he wrote more poems which were collected in *Counter-Attack* (1918).

In 1918, Sassoon returned to active service, first in the Middle East and then in France. On patrol in No Man's Land, he was shot and wounded by one of his own men. In this strange way, he escaped from the Front and survived the war, living on until 1967.

Sassoon's poems aimed to tell the truth about war. He particularly wanted to upset 'blood-thirsty civilians and those who falsely glorified the war'. Memories from France and hints from newspapers would 'bring poems into my head as though from nowhere'. He used a plain, direct style, bringing in soldiers' slang. A pattern of sharp lines often leads to a 'knock-out blow' in the last verse.

An early success was *Died of Wounds*, based on a dying soldier whom he saw in a hospital near the Somme in July 1916.

DIED OF WOUNDS

His wet white face and miserable eyes
Brought nurses to him more than groans and sighs:
But hoarse and low and rapid rose and fell
His troubled voice: he did the business well.

The ward grew dark; but he was still complaining
And calling out for 'Dickie'. 'Curse the Wood!
It's time to go. O Christ, and what's the good?
We'll never take it, and it's always raining.'

I wondered where he'd been; then heard him shout,
'They snipe like hell! O Dickie, don't go out' …
I fell asleep … Next morning he was dead;
And some Slight Wound lay smiling on the bed.

CLOSE STUDY

1   Who was Dickie?

2   Why is the dying man so distressed about him?

3   Which two lines best express the horror and futility of war?

4   What is the sad meaning of the last line?

The Hero is a miniature short story in verse. A 'brother officer' on leave has called to see a bereaved 'Mother', whose son 'Jack' has been killed recently at the Front. The Mother consoles herself by thinking of her son as a hero; the officer knows that Jack was a coward who died miserably – but he does not tell her. Sassoon said that his **satire** was an antidote to the false 'glorification of the "supreme sacrifice".'

THE HERO

'Jack fell as he'd have wished,' the Mother said,
And folded up the letter that she'd read.
'The Colonel writes so nicely.' Something broke
In the tired voice that quavered to a choke.
She half looked up. 'We mothers are so proud
Of our dead soldiers.' Then her face was bowed.

Quietly the Brother Officer went out.
He'd told the poor old dear some gallant lies
That she would nourish all her days, no doubt.
For while he coughed and mumbled, her weak eyes
Had shone with gentle triumph, brimmed with joy,
Because he'd been so brave, her glorious boy.

He thought how 'Jack', cold-footed, useless swine,
Had panicked down the trench that night the mine
Went up at Wicked Corner; how he'd tried
To get sent home, and how, at last, he died,
Blown to small bits. And no one seemed to care
Except that lonely woman with white hair.

CLOSE STUDY

1 How does the Mother behave in stanza 1?

2 How does the officer conduct himself in the interview?

3 How exactly did Jack behave at the Front?

4 In what ways does the officer try to help the Mother?

5 What does he think of her in the last line?

6 What is the **theme** of the poem?

7 Two different styles of **language** divide the characters:
   a) Mother has absorbed the **epic style** used by propagandists (see pp.36-41) that portrayed the war as an epic adventure. 'Fell' is a typical **euphemism** which avoids the harshness of 'died' or 'was killed'. Find other examples of epic language in Mother's words and behaviour.

   b) By contrast, the officer thinks in blunt soldier **slang**. He knows that Jack was 'blown to small bits', using grim humour to describe horror. Find other such **colloquialisms** in stanzas 2 and 3.

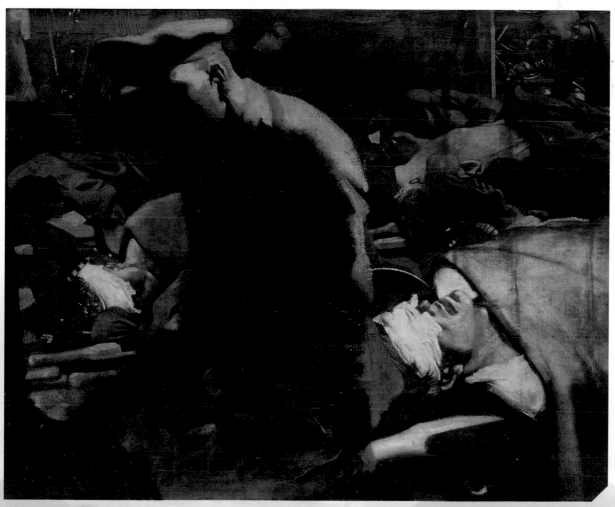

Gassed and Wounded: Eric Kennington

Imagine that you are the 'brother officer'. Write the story of your visit to the Mother while on your leave. Include your memories of Jack as you approach the house, and contrast them with those of Mother in the meeting. What effect does the event have on each of you?

Sassoon resented those who directed the fighting but took no active part in it. On leave in Rouen, he observed a senior officer eating an expensive meal: 'Why can't you go and show the Germans how to fight instead of guzzling at the Base?' This inspired another **satire**, again built around two voices, the observer and the Major.

BASE DETAILS[1]

If I were fierce, and bald, and short of breath,
  I'd live with scarlet Majors at the Base,
And speed glum heroes up the line to death.
  You'd see me with my puffy petulant face
Guzzling and gulping in the best hotel,
  Reading the Roll of Honour. 'Poor young chap',
I'd say – 'I used to know his father well:
  Yes, we've lost heavily in this last scrap.'
And when the war is done and youth stone dead,
I'd toddle safely home and die – in bed.

[1] **Base details:** men who worked at supply depots

CLOSE STUDY

1 What second meaning is included in the title?

2 What does the typical senior officer look like and how does he behave?

3 What two meanings are there in 'scarlet Majors'?

4 What is the point of the last two lines?

5 Sassoon is very good at choosing precise words. Which do you find most vivid?

In *The General*, Sassoon made his classic Great War protest about incompetent military leadership. In only seven **epigrammatic** lines, he sums up the bitterness of the fighting troops about the costly, largely futile Battles of the Somme (1916) and Arras (1917). The **satire** was inspired by Sassoon's observations of the Corps Commander as the Royal Welch Fusiliers marched past him on their way to Arras in April 1917.

THE GENERAL

'Good-morning; good-morning! the General said
When we met him last week on our way to the line.
Now the soldiers he smiled at are most of 'em dead,
And we're cursing his staff for incompetent swine.
'He's a cheery old card,'[1] grunted Harry to Jack
As they slogged up to Arras with rifle and pack.

*

But he did for them both by his plan of attack.

[1] **card:** smart chap

CLOSE STUDY

1 How does the General's greeting contrast with the work that the men are about to do?

2 What happened to the two soldiers? Who was to blame for their fate? Why mention Harry and Jack particularly?

3 The poem ends with three **rhymes**. What is the effect of the long pause before the last rhymed line?

Generals arguing: William Roberts

4 Sassoon uses words from soldiers' **slang** and other **colloquialisms**. Why? Do you think they add to the force of the poem?

5 Why is 'did for them both' better than the 'murdered them both' of the first draft?

Sassoon knew all too well the living death that severe wounds could bring to a man. In a letter of 1917 he told a friend

I hear an R.W.F. (Royal Welch Fusiliers) friend of mine has had an arm amputated, and will probably lose the other. As he was very keen on playing the piano this seems a little hard on him, but no doubt he will be all the better in the end ...

In this poem about civilians' attitudes to badly wounded soldiers, Sassoon uses **sarcasm** to pretend to agree with the civilian speaker of each stanza. He knows that the reality of war wounds is more cruel, though, as it means a lifetime of suffering and people actually fear and dislike the wounded, and want to forget them quickly.

DOES IT MATTER?

Does it matter? – losing your legs? ...
For people will always be kind,
And you need not show that you mind
When the others come in after hunting
To gobble their muffins and eggs.

Does it matter? – losing your sight? ...
There's such splendid work for the blind;
And people will always be kind,
As you sit on the terrace remembering
And turning your face to the light.

Do they matter? – those dreams from the pit? ...
You can drink and forget and be glad,
And people won't say that you're mad;
For they'll know that you've fought for your country
And no one will worry a bit.

CLOSE STUDY

1 What three injuries are described?

2 How has each injury changed the victim's life?

3 What for you is the saddest picture presented in the poem?

4 Sassoon pretends to agree with false civilian attitudes. Which lines show this pretence?

5 What does Sassoon actually mean? Look, for example, at the line 'people will always be kind'.

6 Sassoon uses his favourite **colloquial** style. List some colloquial words and phrases from the poem. What **tone of voice** do these suggest?

Four of the lines in each stanza **rhyme**. One does not: the fourth. This line is also longer. The regular lines have an **anapest metre** (two unstressed **syllables** followed by a stressed one):

u u / u u / u u /
You can drink and forget and be glad

The longer lines have an unstressed syllable at the end. This is called a **feminine ending**.

u u / u u / u u / u
As you sit on the terrace remembering
('-bering' counts as one sound)

7 What is the exact effect of this fade-out line ending and which of the three is most effective?

WRITING

Write three eight line descriptions of the three wounded men. Use details from the poem, and add something from your own imagination. Add a final paragraph expressing your concern for the men and your anger at the war that caused their suffering.

The misery of trench warfare caused men on both sides to kill themselves to escape the fear and stress. Such men died ingloriously by self-inflicted wounds (SIW). Sassoon chooses one such figure, in the poem on the next page, whose individual story is more impressive than sheets of statistics. 'The soldier is no longer a noble figure,' he wrote in his diary. 'He is merely a writing insect among this ghastly folly of destruction.'

SUICIDE IN THE TRENCHES

I knew a simple soldier boy
Who grinned at life in empty joy,
Slept soundly through the lonesome dark,
And whistled early with the lark.

In winter trenches, cowed and glum,
With crumps[1] and lice and lack of rum,[2]
He put a bullet through his brain.
No one spoke of him again.

*   *   *

You smug-faced crowds with kindling[3] eye
Who cheer when soldier lads march by,
Sneak home and pray you'll never know
The hell where youth and laughter go.

[1] **crumps:** *shell bursts*
[2] **rum:** *given to soldiers before attack*
[3] **kindling:** *on fire with enthusiasm*

● CLOSE STUDY

1 How old is the young soldier?

2 What was his attitude to life, making him an unlikely suicide?

3 What were the miseries of trench war that broke his spirit?

4 Why did 'no one speak of him again'?

The focus of the poem shifts to 'smug-faced crowds' at home who are against an end to the fighting.

5 How do these civilian crowds respond to war?

6 What do they not understand about the fighting?

7 What would they think of the suicide victim?

The poem illustrates the power of Sassoon's **diction**.

8 Consider the exact meaning and force of 'empty joy', 'whistled early', 'cowed', 'smug-faced', 'kindling', 'soldier lads', 'sneak home'.

9 The Western Front is 'hell', a man-made nightmare place of torment and horror.

   Why are the **abstract nouns** 'youth' and 'laughter' so impressive beside the word 'hell'?

10 Sassoon uses **pauses** very effectively in this apparently simple poem.

   Think about

   • the effect of the heavy pause after 'brain'
   • the starred gap between stanzas 2 and 3
   • the end-line pause after 'know'.

11 The poem uses conventional **rhymes**. Where are they most effective?

✎ WRITING

Suicide in the Trenches

1 Sassoon stands in a London street watching crowds cheering and men marching past on their way to the Front. He remembers the young soldier he knew who shot himself. Describe the scene, contrasting the reaction of the crowds with Sassoon's thoughts about the crowd and his memories of the trench suicide. Aim for about 500 words.

Some or all of the poems in this section

2 Write an essay on Sassoon's poetic protest against the First World War. You will need a brief introduction (you could use part of his 'protest statement'). Consider the subject matter and **themes** of the poems. Look at the **diction**, **imagery** and **verse forms**, and say how these contribute to the protest. End by saying which poem you find most striking.

Trench suicide: Otto Dix

UNIT 15 //

Wilfred Owen: the pity of war

Wilfred Owen in July 1916

from: THE BALLAD OF PEACE AND WAR

Oh meet it is and passing sweet
    To live at peace with others,
But sweeter still and far more meet[1]
    To die in war for brothers …

The soil is safe, for widow and waif,
    And for the soul of England,
Because their bodies men vouchsafe[2]
    To save the soul of England.

[1] **meet:** *fitting*
[2] **vouchsafe:** *give*

He returned to England to volunteer for the army, telling his mother, 'I now do most intensely want to fight'. After training, he became an officer and was sent to France at the end of 1916, seeing service first in the Somme sector. In spring 1917, he took part in the attacks on the German Hindenburg Line near St Quentin. When a huge shell burst near him, he was shell-shocked and sent back to England.

The horrors of battle had changed him quickly from the youth of August 1914, who had felt that 'the guns will effect a little useful weeding.' Now he wrote to his mother:

Already I have comprehended a light which never will filter into the dogma of any national church: namely that one of Christ's essential commands was: Passivity at any price! Suffer dishonour and disgrace; but never resort to arms. Be bullied, be outraged, be killed: but do not kill.

16 May 1917

Owen was treated at Craiglockhart Hospital in Edinburgh. Doctors there specialized in shell-shock. By day it was cheerful enough but at night the officer patients were tormented by their memories.

Owen is now seen as the most important of the many poets of the First World War. A recent critic says of his poems: 'They speak to our world still, as they were meant to do. … He has done as much as anyone to prevent the reading public from being persuaded ever again that death in battle is "sweet and decorous".'

The son of a railway worker, Owen was born in Shropshire and educated at schools in Shrewsbury and Liverpool. His devoted mother encouraged his early interests in music and poetry. When he could not afford a university education, he went abroad to teach English in France. He was there when war broke out in 1914. He wrote a draft for a war poem that contrasted strangely with his later work. This is part of it.

One lay awake and listened to feet padding along passages which smelt of stale cigarette smoke ... one became conscious that the place was full of men whose slumbers were morbid and terrifying – men muttering uneasily or suddenly crying out in their sleep ... by night each man was back in his doomed sector of a horror-stricken Front Line, where the panic and stampede of some ghastly experience was re-enacted among the livid faces of the dead. No doctor could save him then ...

Siegfried Sassoon, *Sherston's Progress* 1936

Patients were encouraged to return to their pre-war interests. Owen looked over his old poems and began to write new ones. He read Sassoon's *The Old Huntsman* and was deeply impressed. It was a great moment for him when Sassoon himself arrived at the Hospital in August 1917. He plucked up the courage to visit him. Sassoon recalled the first meeting.

One morning at the beginning of August, when I had been at Craiglockhart War Hospital about a fortnight, there was a gentle knock on the door of my room and a young officer entered. Short, dark-haired, and shyly hesitant, he stood for a moment before coming across to the window, where I was sitting on my bed cleaning my golf clubs. A favourable first impression was made by the fact that he had under his arm several copies of *The Old Huntsman*. He had come, he said, hoping that I would be so gracious as to inscribe them for himself and some of his friends. He spoke with a slight stammer, which was no unusual thing in that neurosis-pervaded hospital ...

During the next half-hour or more I must have spoken mainly about my book and its interpretations of the War. He listened eagerly, questioning me with reticent intelligence. It was only when he was departing that he confessed to being a writer of poetry himself, though none of it had yet appeared in print.

It amuses me to remember that, when I had resumed my ruminative club-polishing, I wondered whether his poems were any good! He had seemed an interesting little chap but had not struck me as remarkable. In fact my first view of him was as a rather ordinary young man.

Siegfried Sassoon, *Siegfried's Journey* 1945

Sassoon encouraged Owen in his writing, telling him to 'sweat your guts out writing poetry'. When Owen began to write new poems based on his war experiences, Sassoon helped him to improve and develop his drafts.

Anthem for Doomed Youth was an example of their collaboration.

This **sonnet** was written, with extensive help from Sassoon, in September 1917. In it Owen uses the traditional **Shakespearean sonnet pattern**, rhymed ABAB CDCD EFEF GG. Sassoon commented on it in the following way:

this new sonnet was a revelation ... I now realized that his verse, with its noble naturalness and depth of meaning, had impressive affinities with Keats, whom he took as his supreme exemplar.

Owen protests at the way soldiers are killed on the Western Front. Their deaths can seem as swift and unrecognised as those of cattle in a slaughter house. There seems to be no formal funeral ceremonial attending their deaths. Then he reflects that there are after all equivalents of this ceremonial in the sounds of the Front and the reactions of relatives at home.

ANTHEM FOR DOOMED YOUTH

What passing-bells for these who die as cattle?
  – Only the monstrous anger of the guns.
  Only the stuttering rifles' rapid rattle
Can patter out their hasty orisons.[1]
No mockeries now for them; no prayers nor bells;
  Nor any voice of mourning save the choirs, –
The shrill, demented[2] choirs of wailing shells;
  And bugles calling for them from sad shires.

What candles may be held to speed them all?
  Not in the hands of boys but in their eyes
Shall shine the holy glimmers of goodbyes.
  The pallor of girls' brows shall be their pall;[3]
Their flowers the tenderness of patient[4] minds,
And each slow dusk a drawing-down of blinds.

[1] **orisons:** *prayers*
[2] **demented:** *mad*
[3] **pall:** *cloth to cover coffin*
[4] **patient:** *suffering*

CLOSE STUDY

The poem compares features of the Western Front and reactions of relatives at home to the ceremonial of a funeral.

1   For each of the following features of a funeral, find their counterpart in the poem: prayers; choirs singing; candles round the coffin; pall, and flowers.

2   Which are most appropriate or moving?

3   Does this pattern of **comparisons** seem merely clever or does the *Anthem* remain a powerful **elegy**?

Owen had an acute ear for music and was a master of **onomatopoeia**. For example in the line,

Only the monstrous anger of the guns

the repeated short 'u' sounds suggest the booming of the guns themselves.

4   Find other lines where similar effects are used.

Anthem for Dead Youth.

What passing bells for these who die so fast?
— Only the {monstrous anger of the guns.
Let the blind insolence majestic of their mouths
Be as the priest requiem words of their requiem —
learn choristers and holy music, none;
Nor any voice of mourning, save the wail
Send the long-drawn hiss wail of lonely far-sailing shells.

What candles may we hold for these lost? souls?
— Not in the hands of boys, but in their eyes
shine the candles flames: and will light them.
Shall many flames:
And Women's wide-spread arms shall be their wreaths,
And pallor of girls' cheeks shall be their palls.
Their flowers, the tenderness of mortal minds,
And each slow Dusk, a drawing-down of blinds.

First Draft
(With Sassoon's amendments.)

Draft of *Anthem for Doomed Youth* by Wilfred Owen

Study the two manuscripts chosen from the six drafts of the poem. There are many word / line changes, some done by Sassoon (as in 'doomed' for 'dead' in the title). Discuss the benefits of these changes:

- *so fast > as cattle*
- *solemn > monstrous*
- *music > mockeries*
- *hiss > wailing*
- *disconsolate > demented*
- *rough men's > mortal / silent / patient*
- *every > each slow*

Write a review of this sonnet:

- What is it about?
- What does it tell us about soldiers at the Front and people at home?
- Comment on the language (**diction**, **onomatopoeia**), rhythm and pattern of comparisons.
- Do you think the sonnet form is used effectively?

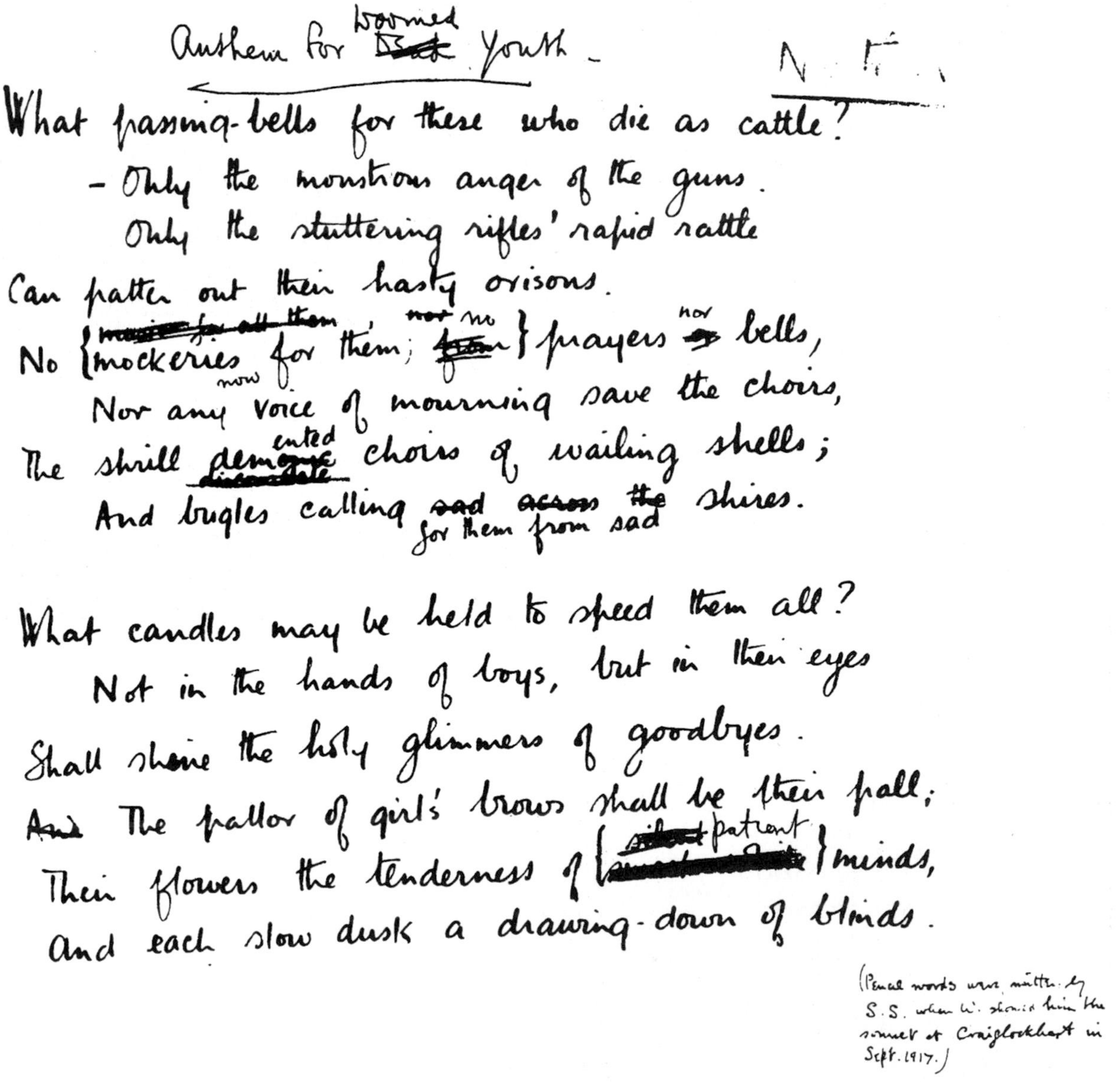

Draft of *Anthem for Doomed Youth* by Wilfred Owen

Another of Owen's Craiglockhart poems was *Dulce et Decorum est*, which has become one of the best-known poems of the twentieth century. In a letter to his mother he wrote:

Here is a gas poem, done yesterday ... The famous Latin tag means of course It is sweet and meet to die for one's country. Sweet! And decorous!

16 October 1917

The 'tag' was from a poem by the Roman poet, Horace, and was much quoted during the days of the British Empire in the nineteenth century, during the Boer War, and also after 1914. Owen attacks the sentimental, bogus patriotism of stay-at-home war enthusiasts: the poem was first addressed to Jessie Pope (see p.38). She is the 'you' of the last section of the poem.

To Owen, the new weaponry of 1914–18 made the Horace epigraph out-of-date. The Romans fought face-to-face with enemies, and the more skilful man won. Now the best and bravest soldier could die horribly in poison gas from a shell fired from five miles away by an invisible, uncaring opponent.

Poison gas, first used as a weapon in April 1915, could be released from cylinders or (as here) fired in shells. Chlorine or phosgene attacked the eyes and lungs, causing 'knife-edge pain ... and the coughing up of greenish froth ... ending in insensibility and death.'

DULCE ET DECORUM EST

Bent double, like old beggars under sacks,
Knock-kneed, coughing like hags, we cursed through
  sludge,
Till on the haunting flares we turned our backs
And towards our distant rest began to trudge.
Men marched asleep. Many had lost their boots
But limped on, blood-shod. All went lame; all blind;
Drunk with fatigue; deaf even to the hoots
Of tired, outstripped Five-Nines[1] that dropped behind.

Gas! GAS! Quick, boys! – An ecstasy of fumbling,
Fitting the clumsy helmets just in time;
But someone still was yelling out and stumbling,
And flound'ring like a man in fire or lime …
Dim, through the misty panes and thick green light,
As under a green sea, I saw him drowning.

In all my dreams, before my helpless sight,
He plunges at me, guttering[2], choking, drowning.

If in some smothering dreams you too could pace
Behind the wagon that we flung him in,
And watch the white eyes writhing in his face,
His hanging face, like a devil's sick of sin;
If you could hear, at every jolt, the blood
Come gargling from the froth-corrupted lungs,
Obscene as cancer, bitter as the cud[3]
Of vile, incurable sores on innocent tongues, –
My friend, you would not tell with such high zest
To children ardent[4] for some desperate glory,
The old Lie: Dulce et decorum est
Pro patria mori.

[1] **Five-Nines:** *shells.*
[2] **guttering:** *flickering and about to go out*
[3] **cud:** *regurgitated food*
[4] **ardent:** *eager*

The gas chamber (detail): William Roberts.

Dulce et Decorum est.

To Jessie Pope etc. To a certain Poetess.

Bent double, like old beggars under sacks,
Knock-kneed, coughing like hags, we cursed through sludge,
Till on the ~~glowing~~ *haunting* flares we turned our backs,
And towards our distant rest began to trudge.
Dead slow we moved. Many had lost their boots,
But limped on, blood-shod. All went lame; all blind;
Drunk with fatigue; deaf even to the hoots
~~Of disappointed shells that dropped behind.~~
Of ~~tired-voiced~~ *five-nines* that dropped behind.
~~the outstripped~~

Then somewhere near in front: Whew... fup... fop... fup...
Gas-shells or duds? We loosened masks, in case —
And listened.... Nothing.... Far rumouring of Krupp...
Then ~~smartly~~ *stinging*, poison hit us in the face.
Gas! GAS! ~~An ecstasy of~~ *Quick, boys!* — An ecstasy of fumbling,?
Fitting the clumsy helmets just in time.
But someone still was yelling out, and stumbling,
And floundering like a man in fire or lime. —
Dim, through the misty panes and thick green light,
As under a dark sea, I saw him drowning.

In all my dreams, before my helpless sight,
He ~~plunges~~ *plunges* at me, ~~guttering~~, choking, drowning.
~~gurgling~~
~~gaggling~~
~~guttering~~

In ~~all your~~ *If too the smother of some smoke* dreams, my friend, if you too could pace
Behind the ~~limber~~ *wagon* that we flung him in,
And watch the white eyes ~~turning~~ *writhing* in his face,
His hanging face, like a devil's sick of sin; —
If you could hear, at every jolt, the blood
Come gargling from the froth-~~corroded~~ *corrupted* lungs,
~~And think how, once, his head was like a bud,~~
~~Obscene a 'cancer'~~ *tense*
~~Fresh as a country rose, and keen, and young,~~
You'd not repeat with such a noble zest,
To children ardent for some desperate glory,
The old Lie: Dulce et decorum est
Pro patria mori.

Of ~~a kill~~ incurable sores ~~on innocent~~ bitter as the cud longues
My friend, you would not tell with such high zest
∇ To children

Draft of Dulce et Decorum est by Wilfred Owen

⬤ **CLOSE STUDY**

Section 1

Owen describes a group of soldiers leaving the front line trenches after a spell of duty there. Exhausted and unkempt, they are walking to a rest area.

1   What state are they in (exactly)?

2   Which two surprising **comparisons** describe the soldiers?

3   What is the grim joke of 'blood-shod'?

4   What happens in the last line of this section?

5   Owen selects ugly, textured, guttural **diction** to convey a hideous event and landscape. 'Sludge' is one such word. Find others in the first four lines.

Sections 2 and 3 (two lines)

Chlorine or phosgene gas flows from the shells. The men put on their gas masks.

6   Why is 'GAS' repeated in capitals?

7   Explain the phrases 'an ecstasy of fumbling', and 'the misty panes'.

8   Three **comparisons** describe the horrible fate of one man. What are these? What effect does the dying man have on the narrator?

9   What does 'plunges at me' mean? What does 'guttering' mean exactly?

10   Explore the force of the words: 'flound'ring', 'fire', 'lime', 'guttering', and the underwater comparison (gas has green fumes).

Section 4

This is one long sentence addressed to 'my friend', the war enthusiast in England, ending with a bitter attack on the 'old lie': that it is glorious to die for your country.

11   What do the soldiers do with the dying man?

12   The man's face hangs upside down. What horrible details of the face are given to us, and with what is it compared?

13   The gas eats away the man's lungs. Which ugly words and **comparisons** describe this result?

14   Who are the children and what is 'some desperate glory'?

15   Look closely at the horrible details and think about their meaning and force: 'writhing', 'hanging', 'devil', 'froth-corrupted', 'cud', 'sores'.

DISCUSSION

Read the draft manuscript and compare it with the final version looking particularly at

haunting rather than *clawing*

guttering rather than *gurgling*

the completely recast sections

the comparison of the dead man's face to a rose.

Did the changes benefit the poem?

WRITING

1   Recast the material of the poem into a letter written by the narrator to a friend at home who is an enthusiast for war. Try to include the 'story' of the poem, its angry theme, and some of the force and indignation of its language. The purpose of your writing will be the same as Owen's. Aim for roughly 500 words.

2   Write a critical commentary on this poem, discussing its

   • subject matter
   • angry **theme**
   • **imagery**
   • linguistic and stylistic effects

3   Write a script based on the meeting of Wilfred Owen and Siegfried Sassoon. They might discuss their own backgrounds, the war and their parts in it, and their poems. Include in this a discussion of *Anthem for Doomed Youth* using the manuscripts given on pages 75-76.

Gas attack: Otto Dix

When he left Craiglockhart in October 1917, Owen was declared fit for home service. In spring 1918 he was posted to Ripon in Yorkshire, where he rented a room in a cottage near the camp:

It is a jolly retreat. There I have tea and contemplate the inwardness of war ...

Letter: 31 March 1918

In this room, he wrote some of his finest war poems, beginning *Spring Offensive* (see p.58) and completing *Futility*, published in *The Nation* in June – one of the few poems that Owen ever saw in print. The poem may be based on Owen's first spell of duty in the trenches in January 1917: 'One of my party actually froze to death before he could be got back'; or the dead man may have been a sudden casualty shot down by a sniper at dawn. The poem begins with the crazy order to put the body in the sunshine: somehow the sun might bring him back to life.

FUTILITY[1]

Move him into the sun –
Gently its touch awoke him once,
At home, whispering of fields half-sown.
Always it woke him, even in France,
Until this morning and this snow.
If anything might rouse him now
The kind old sun will know.

Think how it wakes the seeds –
Woke once the clays of a cold star.
Are limbs, so dear achieved, are sides
Full-nerved, still warm, too hard to stir?
Was it for this the clay grew tall?
– O what made fatuous sunbeams toil
To break earth's sleep at all?

[1] *futility: pointlessness*

🔵 **CLOSE STUDY**

1 What work did the dead soldier do before the war? Why, therefore, should the sun wake him?

2 'Fields half-sown': what point is made here about the man, his life, and his work?

3 The 'kind old sun' is the centre of the poem. What wonderful things has it given life to on the 'cold star' (planet Earth)?

4 Owen looks closely at the dead man. Why are his limbs 'dear achieved'?

5 The body is 'still warm' and 'full-nerved': why do these lines give Owen a kind of hope?

6 In the line, 'Was it for this the clay grew tall?', Owen is thinking of the Biblical story of Adam's creation: 'Then the Lord formed a man from the dust of the ground'. What, then, does this line mean?

7 Realizing that the man is finally, hopelessly dead, there is a marked change in **mood** in the final two lines. Comment on how the mood changes. Explain the meaning of the final question.

8 Do you like the **half-rhymes** in this poem? Why does Owen use them here?

9 Having looked at these details, think about the whole poem. What does Owen feel about the death of this man?

First draft of *Futility*: Owen's manuscript, *Frustration*.

✏ WRITING

1   Write a commentary on this poem. What happens in it? What are Owen's thoughts about what happens? What features of the poem – words, comparisons, shape – do you find interesting?

2   Look at the painting below by William Orpen called *A Death Among the Wounded in the Snow*. Write a story or description based on it. Try to bring in thoughts and ideas from Owen's *Futility*.

💬 DISCUSSION

Compare the final version with the draft of *Futility* entitled, *Frustration*. Why has Owen made each change? How has he improved the poem?

The 1918 German March offensive broke the Western Front. As the Germans advanced, every man was needed. Owen returned to France in August and went on to win the Military Cross in September.

On 4 November, at dawn, while men of his Manchester Regiment were trying to cross the Sambre Canal near Ors, Wilfred Owen was shot and killed. A week later, on 11 November, when the Great War ended at 11 a.m., news of his death reached his family. Friends heard later: one concluded sadly that he 'had disappeared into the grey mists of those autumnal regions which had swallowed so many lives'.

A Death Among the Wounded in the Snow: William Orpen

UNIT 16 // Anger and satire

Protest poets had extraordinary freedom in 1914-18. Government censors might suppress prose works or make life difficult for pacifist journals, but civilian and soldier poets spoke freely. Anger was one of their weapons but satire was even more deadly – a bitter, mocking humour directed at authority, armchair warriors, lying propagandists, or the insanity and waste of war itself.

From the first, socialist periodicals like *The Herald* or *The Labour Leader* published such verses:

> "Thou shalt not kill" makes murder sin –
>   No man may slay his brother –
> But men do well, if for the state
>   They maim and kill each other.

The Labour Leader: 14 October 1914

Socialists felt that working people across Europe were united in their struggle to win a better life from their masters. Even the 'fire and pestilence of European war' could not divide them.

> 'Out of the darkness and the depths we hail our working class comrades of every land. Across the roar of guns we send our greeting to German socialists ... They are no enemies of ours.'

Independent Labour Party manifesto: 13 August 1914

It was in this spirit that W.N. Ewer wrote his best-known poem, published on 3 October 1914. He sees the working men of Europe as victims of propaganda.

Armies devoured by the monstrous god of war: Protest cartoon by Joseph Southall

FIVE SOULS

FIRST SOUL

I was a peasant of the Polish plain;
I left my plough because the message ran:
Russia, in danger, needed every man
To save her from the Teuton;[1] and was slain.
I gave my life for freedom – This I know
For those who bade me fight had told me so.

SECOND SOUL

I was a Tyrolese, a mountaineer;
I gladly left my mountain home to fight
Against the brutal treacherous Muscovite;
And died in Poland on a Cossack spear.
I gave my life for freedom – This I know
For those who bade me fight had told me so.

THIRD SOUL

I worked in Lyons at my weaver's loom,
When suddenly the Prussian despot[2] hurled
His felon blow at France and at the world;
Then I went forth to Belgium and my doom.
I gave my life for freedom – This I know
For those who bade me fight had told me so.

FOURTH SOUL

I owned a vineyard by the wooded Main,
Until the Fatherland, begirt[3] by foes
Lusting her downfall, called me, and I rose
Swift to the call – and died in far Lorraine.
I gave my life for freedom – This I know
For those who bade me fight had told me so.

FIFTH SOUL

I worked in a great shipyard by the Clyde;
There came a sudden word of wars declared,
Of Belgium, peaceful, helpless, unprepared,
Asking our aid; I joined the ranks, and died.
I gave my life for freedom – This I know
For those who bade me fight had told me so.

W.N. EWER

[1] **Teuton:** *German*
[2] **despot:** *cruel ruler*
[3] **begirt:** *surrounded*

CLOSE STUDY

1   What is the effect of the repeated **chorus** in each verse?

2   Which words from official propaganda does Ewer put into the mouths of his working men?

3   Who, in Ewer's opinion, are the real enemies of these men?

4   Do you agree, or disagree, with the poet?

Strong Christian believers also opposed war. Alfred Salter, a brilliant London preacher, put this idea in a famous article:

> 'Look! Christ in khaki, thrusting his bayonet into the body of a German workman. See! The Son of God with a machine-gun. Hark! The Man of Sorrows in a cavalry charge, cutting, hacking, thrusting… That settles the matter for me. I cannot uphold the war.

The Labour Leader: 24 September 1914

In Mark Gertler's protest painting, *The Merry-go-round* (1916), war-crazed civilians and soldiers circle pointlessly, chanting crude patriotic slogans

Harold Begbie, a convinced Christian, lost his early enthusiasm for the war (see p.37). He came to detest the attitudes of the right-wing press, especially the notion that war was 'good' for people.

WAR EXALTS

War exalts and cleanses: it lifts man from the mud!
Ask God what He thinks of a bayonet dripping blood.

By War the brave are tested, and cowards are disgraced!
Show God His own image shrapnel'd into paste.

Fight till tyrants perish, slay till brutes are mild!
Then go wash the blood off and try to face your child.

HAROLD BEGBIE

● CLOSE STUDY

1 Each stanza consists of a statement praising war, and an answer attacking it. Put the statements and Begbie's answers into your own words.

2 His answers are blunt and vivid. Which do you find most striking?

"To your health civilization!": in this cartoon by Louis Raemaekers, Death celebrates the slaughter of 1916 with a toast drunk in blood.

War fever reached a new intensity in 1916. Conscription now forced men into the army. The novelist D.H. Lawrence commented,

> It seems as if we are all going to be dragged into the danse macabre (the dance of death). Now it is dance ... to the sound of the knuckle bones.

Letter: 26 April 1916

In a tiny poem, Israel Zangwill, poet and novelist, summed up the spirit of this dark year.

1916

The world bloodily-minded,
    The church dead or polluted,
The blind leading the blinded,
    And the deaf dragging the muted.

ISRAEL ZANGWILL

● CLOSE STUDY

1 What does 'The church dead or polluted' mean?

2 The 'blind', 'deaf', and 'muted' are not war wounded.

   Who, then, are the 'blind' and the 'blinded'? Who are the 'deaf'?

3 In what sense are the 'muted' silent?

4 What does Zangwill find most disturbing about the world of 1916?

Between July and November, 95,675 British soldiers died on the Somme. Thousands more were wounded. Such huge casualties brought the first serious protest from soldier poets. Leslie Coulson, killed in October, left a despairing poem among his effects

from: WHO MADE THE LAW?

Who made the law that men should die in meadows?
Who spake the word that blood should splash in lanes?
Who gave it forth that gardens should be bone-yards?
Who spread the hills with flesh, and blood, and brains?

LESLIE COULSON

Sniping was a deadly skill that might be relished by a marksman as a grim sport. A young officer, Ivar Campbell, described one at work:

> No sign of humanity ... a dead land ... Then, as a rabbit in the early morning comes out to crop grass, a German stepped over the enemy trench, the only living thing in sight. "I'll take him," says the man near me. And like a rabbit he falls ...

Letter: 1915

A Scottish soldier poet W.D. Cocker discussed the implications of such cold-blooded killing in *The Sniper* (1917).

☑ CLOSE STUDY

1   Which words tell us of the sniper's reaction to the killing?

2   Comment on the **rhythm** of the poem, especially when it describes the shooting.

3   The poet imagines the dead German. What do we hear about the appearance of the dead man?

4   The victim's comrades mourn his death. How will the 200 yard shot have results 200 miles away as well?

5   What would happen to the sniper if he thought about this?

6   The poem ends with a clever moral. What is this?

THE SNIPER

Two hundred yards away he saw his head;
  He raised his rifle, took quick aim and shot him.
Two hundred yards away the man dropped dead;
With bright exulting eye he turned and said,
  'By Jove, I got him!'
And he was jubilant;[1] had he not won
  The meed[2] of praise his comrades haste to pay?
He smiled; he could not see what he had done;
  The dead man lay two hundred yards away.
He could not see the dead, reproachful eyes,
  The youthful face which Death had not defiled
But had transfigured when he claimed his prize.
  Had he seen this perhaps he had not smiled.
He could not see the woman as she wept
  To hear the news two hundred miles away,
Or through his every dream she would have crept.
  And into all his thoughts by night and day.
Two hundred yards away, and, bending o'er
  A body in a trench, rough men proclaim
Sadly, that Fritz, the merry, is no more.
  (Or shall we call him Jack? *It's all the same.*)

W.D. COCKER

[1] **jubilant:** *rejoicing*
[2] **meed:** *reward*

Wounded, Bapaume on the Somme, 1916: Otto Dix

In 1917–18 opinion about the war was sharply divided. Many felt that a negotiated peace should end the slaughter, but 'Fight to a finish' enthusiasts believed in 'The battle, the battle: nothing else counts'. In this climate, **satire** grew sharper. Edward Garnett, a prose satirist, wrote a typical piece:

What a wonderful time the Creatures of Blood were having all over Europe! Never in the story of man ... had there been such slaughter, havoc, massacre, insanity, famine and the abomination of desolation on this planet, on as gigantic a scale, as in these glorious years ... The Creatures of Blood in every belligerent country, who had so long grown fat on peace and still supped on plenty, rubbed their white podgy hands, while their bloodshot elderly eyes glanced through the newspapers which bawled night and morning everywhere for bigger and bigger armies to wade deeper and deeper into the morass of European slaughter ...

Papa's War and Other Essays 1918

A French cartoon showing the Kaiser as a butcher dealing in the flesh of men killed on the Western Front.

One theme, explored by many writers, including Owen and Sassoon, was that the older generation was sacrificing the younger to protect its own wealth and comfort. The journalist Philip Gibbs wrote of

a great carving of human flesh which was our boyhood, while the old men directed their sacrifice, and the profiteers grew rich, and the flames of hate were stoked up in editorial chairs.

Realities of war 1920

Louis Golding's *The New Trade* is a **grotesque** poem on this theme. He worked with the Friends' (Quakers) Ambulance Service on various fronts and saw the effects of battle. His fierce poems were published in the anti-war journal *The Cambridge Magazine*, where Sassoon's poems were first published.

THE NEW TRADE

In the market-place they have made
A dolorous[1] new trade.
Now you will see in the fierce naphtha[2] light,
Piled hideously to sight,
Dead limbs of men bronzed in the over-seas,
Bomb-wrenched from elbows and knees;
Torn feet that would, unwearied by harsh loads,
Have tramped steep moorland roads;
Torn hands that would have moulded exquisitely
Rare things for God to see;
And there are eyes there – blue like blue dove's wings,
Black like the Libyan kings,
Grey as before-dawn rivers, willow-stirred;
Brown as a nesting bird;
But all stare from the dark into the dark,
Reproachful, tense and stark.
Eyes heaped on trays and in broad baskets there,
Feet, hands and ropes of hair.
In the market-places ... and women buy ...
... Naphtha glares ... hawkers cry ...
Fat men rub hands
    ... O God, O just God, send
Plagues, lightnings
    ... make an end!

LOUIS GOLDING

[1] **dolorous:** *sorrowful*
[2] **naptha:** *flare used to light market stalls*

CLOSE STUDY

1   Which details do you find most **grotesque**?

2   Which people are the targets of Golding's anger here?

3   What does Golding find so tragic about war casualties?

4   What is the meaning of his last angry outburst?

5   What is the point of this poem?

The victorious battles of 1917–18 were fought on a huge scale. Millions of rounds of gas shells might be fired, as ground-attack aircraft swarmed above hundreds of tanks. An anonymous officer writing to another anti-war journal, *The Nation* (where Wilfred Owen first appeared in print), described the scene:

> Leprous earth scattered with the swollen and blackened corpses of hundreds of young men … Men screaming and gibbering. Wounded men hanging in agony on the barbed wire, until a friendly spout of liquid fire shrivels them up like a fly in a candle.

The Nation 23 June 1917

The gallant individuals of 1914 were now too often 'cannon-fodder'.

Alec Waugh, brother of the novelist Evelyn, fought in France and was taken prisoner. In this angry poem, he looks at the death of a friend and the effects of this on himself and on people at home.

CANNON-FODDER

Is it seven days you've been lying there
   Out in the cold,
Feeling the damp, chill circlet of flesh
   Loosen its hold
On muscles and sinews and bones,
   Feeling them slip
One from the other to hang, limp on the stones?
Seven days. The lice must be busy in your hair,
And by now the worms will have had their share
   Of eyelid and lip.
Poor, lonely thing; is death really a sleep?
Or can you somewhere feel the vermin creep
   Across your face
As you lie, rotting, uncared for in the unowned place,
That you fought so hard to keep
   Blow after weakening blow.
Well. You've got what you wanted, that spot is yours.
No one can take it from you now.

But at home by the fire, their faces aglow
   With talking of you,
They'll be sitting, the folk that you loved,
   And they will not know.

O Girl at the window combing your hair
   Get back to your bed.
   Your bright-limbed lover is lying out there
   Dead.

O mother, sewing by candlelight,
   Put away that stuff.
The clammy fingers of earth are about his neck.
   He is warm enough.

Soon, like a snake in your honest home
   The word will come.

And the light will suddenly go from it.
   Day will be dumb.
And the heart in each aching breast
   Will be cold and numb.

O men, who had known his manhood and truth,
   I had found him true.
O you, who had loved his laughter and youth,
   I had loved it too.
O girl, who has lost the meaning of life,
   I am lost as you.

And yet there is one worse thing,
For all the pain at the heart and the eye blurred and dim,
This you are spared,
You have not seen what death has made of him.

You have not seen the proud limbs mangled and
   broken,
The face of the lover sightless and raw and red,
You have not seen the flock of vermin swarming
   Over the newly dead.

Slowly he'll rot in the place where no man dare go,
Silently over the right the stench[1] of his carcase will flow,
Proudly the worms will be banqueting …
   This you can never know.

He will live in your dreams for ever as last you saw him.
Proud-eyed and clean, a man whom shame never
   knew,
Laughing, erect, with the strength of the wind in his
   manhood –
   O broken-hearted mother, I envy you.

ALEC WAUGH

[1] **stench:** *ugly smell*

CLOSE STUDY

1 What is horrifying about the first stanza?

2 What is the force of his question, 'Is death really a sleep?'

3 The soldier fought hard to stop the enemy taking the ground where he was placed. What is now so sad about that patch of ground?

Waugh imagines the people at home who loved the young soldier.

4 Comment on how the poet describes the news of the man's death in the fifth stanza.

5 What does he want to tell them about his dead friend?

6 At the end of the poem he sees the people at home as being luckier than he is. Why exactly is this? What horror are they spared? What picture in the mind can they keep which the poet cannot?

7 Comment on where you think the **form** of the poem and its **conversation-like style** prove most effective.

WRITING

1 Write your own verse or prose piece entitled Cannon-fodder. You could use the poem and picture to give you some ideas. You might choose to write as a soldier and survivor reviewing a recent attack. Like Waugh, try to suggest the extent of the consequences, both on the soldiers themselves and on the people back home. Use figurative language and the structure of your piece to create effects.

2 Read over the poems in this section. Write about some or all of them.

• What are the targets for their anger?

• What methods do the poets use in their writing to attack their targets?

• Which poems are most successful?

• What do you think of the poems and their subject-matter?

DISCUSSION

Look over the illustrations in this section.

• Exactly what are the artists trying to say in each picture?

• How do the pictures relate to the poems?

• Which medium – words or painting/drawing – is more forceful?

Gassed: Gilbert Rogers

UNIT 17 //

Isaac Rosenberg: Dead man's dump

Isaac Rosenberg, an obscure army private, disappeared on 1 April 1918, during the chaos following the great German March offensive on the Western Front. Not until 1926 could the authorities tell his family that his body had been found, and even now it is possible that the remains buried beneath his headstone, marked with the Jewish star and the inscription 'Artist and poet', are not actually Rosenberg's.

This wretched end seemed a fitting climax to what seemed a dismal, restricted life. The son of Lithuanian Jewish immigrants to London's East End, Rosenberg escaped briefly from the poverty of his boyhood to enjoy (thanks to a wealthy Jewish patron) two years studying painting and writing poems at the Slade School of Art. Yet when war came in 1914, he was trapped again.

Although he 'despised and hated war', he volunteered for the army in 1915. Small, absent-minded and clumsy, he soon found that 'nobody but a private knows what it is to be a slave'. He served nearly two years (with just 10 days' leave) at the Front where, he wrote, 'death seems to underlie even our underthoughts'. Somehow he continued to create, sending poems home in letters even after an officer censor refused to read 'such rubbish'. He told a friend at home

> I am determined that this war, with all its powers for devastation, shall not master my poeting ... I will saturate myself with the strange and extraordinary new conditions of this life, and it will all refine itself into poetry later.

Letter: autumn 1916

His poem *Dead man's dump* began with a real experience:

> I've written some lines suggested by ... carrying wire up the line on limbers and running over dead bodies lying about ... When I work on it, I'll make it fine ...

Letter: 8 May 1917

Dumps of dead soldiers awaiting burial were commonplace near the Front. Henri Barbusse, the French soldier-novelist, described such a dump in his novel *Le feu (Under Fire)* (1917), which so influenced Sassoon and Owen.

> 'Where withered grass is embedded in black mud, there are rows of the dead ... There are some with half mouldy faces, the skin rusty or yellow with dark spots. Of several the faces are black as tar ... between two bodies ... is a severed wrist, ending with a cluster of strings ... Around the dead flutter letters ... I stoop and read a sentence – "My dearest Henry, what a fine day it is for your birthday!"'

Le feu: Chapter 12

Barbusse is angry about the degradation of human life in war; Rosenberg's response is more thoughtful and **elegiac**.

DEAD MAN'S DUMP

The plunging limbers[1] over the shattered track
Racketed with their rusty freight,
Stuck out like many crowns of thorns,
And the rusty stakes like sceptres old
To stay the flood of brutish men
Upon our brothers dear.

The wheels lurched over sprawled dead
But pained them not, though their bones crunched,
Their shut mouths made no moan,
They lie there huddled, friend and foeman,
Man born of man, and born of woman,
And shells go crying over them
From night till night and now.

Earth has waited for them
All the time of their growth
Fretting for their decay:
Now she has them at last!
In the strength of their strength
Suspended – stopped and held.

What fierce imaginings their dark souls lit
Earth! have they gone into you?
Somewhere they must have gone,
And flung on your hard back
Is their souls' sack,
Emptied of God-ancestralled[2] essences.
Who hurled them out? Who hurled?

None saw their spirits' shadow shake the grass,
Or stood aside for the half used life to pass
Out of those doomed nostrils and the doomed mouth,
When the swift iron burning bee[3]
Drained the wild honey of their youth.

What of us, who flung on the shrieking pyre,
Walk, our usual thoughts untouched,
Our lucky limbs as on ichor[4] fed,
Immortal seeming ever?
Perhaps when the flames beat loud on us,
A fear may choke in our veins
And the startled blood may stop.

The air is loud with death,
The dark air spurts with fire
The explosions ceaseless are.

Timelessly now, some minutes past,
These dead strode time with vigorous life,
Till the shrapnel called 'an end!'
But not to all. In bleeding pangs
Some borne on stretchers dreamed of home,
Dear things, war-blotted from their hearts.

A man's brains splattered on
A stretcher-bearer's face;
His shook shoulders slipped their load,
But when they bent to look again
The drowning soul was sunk too deep
For human tenderness.

They left this dead with the older dead,
Stretched at the cross roads.

Burnt black by strange decay,
Their sinister faces lie
The lid over each eye,
The grass and coloured clay
More motion have than they,
Joined to the great sunk silences.

Here is one not long dead;
His dark hearing caught our far wheels,
And the choked soul stretched weak hands
To reach the living word the far wheels said,
The blood-dazed intelligence beating for light,
Crying through the suspense of the far torturing wheels
Swift for the end to break,
Or the wheels to break,
Cried as the tide of the world broke over his sight.

Will they come? Will they ever come?
Even as the mixed hoofs of the mules,
The quivering-bellied mules,
And the rushing wheels all mixed
With his tortured upturned sight,
So we crashed round the bend,
We heard his weak scream,
We heard his very last sound,
And our wheels grazed his dead face.

ISAAC ROSENBERG

---

[1] **limbers:** *supply carts*
[2] **God-ancestralled:** *created by God*
[3] **iron bee:** *bullet*
[4] **ichor:** *blood of the gods*

CLOSE STUDY

Section 1: The plunging limbers ... brothers dear

Rosenberg describes the noisy journey of the supply cart loaded with barbed wire and metal stakes for the wire fence.

1   Which words suggest the movement and noise of the cart?

2   The wire looks like 'crowns of thorns'. Why is this **simile** so appropriate here?

3   In another **simile**, the stakes are compared to the sceptres of ancient kings, like Canute who thought he could hold back the tide. Comment on this image and the **metaphor** of the 'flood'. Who are the 'brutish men' and the 'brothers dear'?

Section 2: The wheels ... honey of their youth

As the cart runs over dead bodies, the poet reflects on the mysterious change from life to death in these men from both sides. 'Man born of woman' is a reminder of the Christian burial service.

4   What mourning does the battlefield seem to provide for the dead soldiers?

5   Earth is often **personified** as a kindly mother. How is it seen very differently here?

6   In which two lines does Rosenberg picture the instant of death?

7   The poet respects the God-created wonders of life in human beings. Find three **phrases** that describe these.

8   Which two words bluntly portray the body after death?

9   Comment on the **language** and use of **sibilance** to describe the soul leaving the dying body.

Section 3: What of us ... human tenderness

Rosenberg thinks about the living and the dead on the battlefield.

10   The living are amazed and happy to survive somehow. Which words tell you this?

11   Which three lines give more detail of the 'shrieking pyre' that is the battlefield?

12   What do the dying men dream of as they lie on stretchers?

13   One man is hit again as he is carried away: horribly his 'brains splatter' on the stretcher-bearer. Comment on the **metaphor** used in the last two lines.

Section 4: They left this dead ... sunk silences

14   What idea is suggested by 'stretched at the crossroads'?

15   What is ugly and strange about the appearance of dead men at the dump?

16   Why mention the 'grass' and 'coloured clay'?

17   The dead men join the countless millions of humans who have died before them. Which three words convey this vision of death?

Section 5: Here is one ... his dead face

Rosenberg shifts viewpoint from his own to that of a dying soldier who hears the cart in the distance and longs for it to arrive. By the time it reaches him, he is already dead.

18   Which words and **phrases** suggest his closeness to death?

19   Comment on how Rosenberg creates suspense as the cart nears the dying man.

20   What is **ironic** and sad about the last three lines?

DISCUSSION

1   The poem is a blend of quiet reflection on the mystery of life and death, and of hideous violence. Find and discuss the effect of lines which express these contrasts.

2   Siegfried Sassoon loved Rosenberg's language, which he called 'impassioned expression' with 'a sinewy and muscular aliveness'. It is a mixture of **epic** grandeur and bold, almost **colloquial**, simplicity. Choose eight lines, or line groups, that you like. Try to explain what they are about and why you find them powerful.

WRITING

1   Continue the letter to a friend (8 May 1917) that is quoted in the introduction to this section. Describe his experience on the way to, and at, the dump in full, and what he thought and felt about the dead men he saw.

2 Fred Varley, a Canadian war artist, painted this picture, *For what?* of dead soldiers awaiting burial. When he left the war zone, he wrote to a friend:

> *I'm mighty thankful I've left France ... I'm going to paint a picture of it but heavens ... we'd be healthier to forget, and that we never can. We are for ever tainted with its abortiveness and cruel drama ...*

Letter: May 1919

What can you see in the picture? Describe its details and colours carefully. Then compare it with Rosenberg's poem. Discuss which makes more impact in its portrayal of life and death in war.

COMPARING POEMS

Rosenberg's *Dead man's dump* and *Spring offensive* by Wilfred Owen (see p.58) are often seen as the masterpieces of these great soldier poets. They share similar themes of life and death, and display contrasting moods of reflection and sudden violence.

Compare the poems, thinking about

- the 'stories' that they tell
- their depiction of living and dying in war
- their diction, imagery and style.

Burying the dead on a bleak battlefield: *For what?*: Fred Varley

UNIT 18 //

Armistice and after

The First World War ended by an Armistice at 11 a.m. on 11 November 1918. The tidy style of the eleventh hour of the eleventh day of the eleventh month appealed to the military mind of the time. A soldier remembered what it was like on that day at the Front when peace finally came.

Edward Plunkett, Lord Dunsany, was wounded at the Somme in 1916. His sonnet, *A Dirge of Victory*, shows no sense of pleasure or triumph at the defeat of Germany. A dirge is, in fact, a poem of sadness and mourning.

> At a few minutes before eleven o'clock we all went to where the guns were, drawn up in a line behind a hedge … All the guns fired. This was the first time I had heard our guns firing blank ammunition. The noise was no more than a bang, and puffs of white smoke hung over the muzzles of the guns and drifted slowly away. Some of the men started to cheer, but their voices sounded as unnatural as the noise of the guns, and they soon stopped. There was silence. It had come to stay …

P.J. Campbell, *The Ebb and Flow of Battle* 1979

A DIRGE OF VICTORY

Lift not thy trumpet, Victory, to the sky,
   Nor through battalions nor by batteries blow,
   But over hollows full of old wire go,
Where, among dregs of war, the long-dead lie
With wasted iron that the guns passed by
   When they went eastward like a tide at flow;
   There blow thy trumpet that the dead may know,
Who waited for thy coming, Victory.

It is not we that have deserved thy wreath.
   They waited there among the towering weeds:
The deep mud burned under the thermite's[1] breath,
   And winter cracked the bones that no man heeds:
Hundreds of nights flamed by: the seasons passed.
And thou hast come to them at last, at last!

LORD DUNSANY

[1] **thermite:** *explosive*

Armistice night, 1918: William Roberts

Victory is often represented as a goddess blowing a trumpet of triumph.

1 Which people should she seek out and celebrate with at the war's end?

2 Describe the place where these people are.

3 Why, in the poet's opinion, is it appropriate that Victory visits them?

4 How does the **sestet** suggest how Victory's visit was anticipated over time?

5 Comment on the choice of the **sonnet** form and how its **structure** and **rhyme** scheme have been exploited by the poet.

May Cannan was working in a British government office in Paris when the war ended. She describes the atmosphere of this office when the news came through and the effect that the Armistice had on the girls working there. (Her soldier fiancé survived the fighting only to die tragically in the 'Spanish influenza' pandemic in February 1919).

'And knew that peace could not give her back her dead'

THE ARMISTICE

The news came through over the telephone:
All the terms had been signed: the War was won:
And all the fighting and the agony,
And all the labour of the years were done.

One girl clicked sudden at her typewriter
And whispered, 'Jerry's safe,' and sat and stared:
One said, 'It's over, over, it's the end:
The War is over: ended': and a third,
'I can't remember life without the war'.
And one came in and said, 'Look here, they say
We can all go at five to celebrate,
As long as two stay on, just for today'.

It was quite quiet in the big empty room
Among the typewriters and little piles
Of index cards: one said, 'We'd better just
Finish the day's reports and do the files'.
And said, 'It's awf'lly like *Recessional*[1],
Now when the tumult has all died away'.
The other said, 'Thank God we saw it through:
I wonder what they'll do at home today'.
And said, 'You know it will be quiet tonight
Up at the Front: first time in all these years,
And no one will be killed there any more',
And stopped, to hide her tears.
She said, 'I've told you; he was killed in June'.
The other said, 'My dear, I know; I know …
It's over for me too … My man was killed,
Wounded … and died … at Ypres … three years
   ago …
And he's my man, and I want him,' she said,
And knew that peace could not give back her dead.

MAY WEDDERBURN CANNAN

[1] ***Recessional:*** *poem by Rudyard Kipling*

1 Why does the writer not give any of the girls' names?

2 What are their immediate reactions to the news?

3 What are their later reactions, when the news has sunk in?

4 This poem has real **atmosphere**. Which details, especially of sounds, create this?

In the first years after the war, Armistice Day was celebrated with careful ceremonial. The two minutes' silence was taken literally: traffic stopped and people stood still, bare-headed in the streets, remembering the dead. By 1921, the wartime industrial boom was over. As depression and unemployment grew, Prime Minister Lloyd George's promise 'to make Britain a fit country for heroes to live in' began to seem hollow. One ex-soldier recalled the problems of peace.

> Although an expert machine-gunner, I was a numbskull so far as any trade or craft was concerned ... and I joined the queues for jobs as messengers, window-cleaners and scullions. It was a complete let-down for thousands like me, and for some young officers, too. It was a common sight in London to see ex-officers with barrel-organs endeavouring to earn a living as beggars ...

George Coppard, *With a Machine-gun to Cambrai* 1969

Edward Shanks brings this disillusion into his poem about the Cenotaph ceremony.

CLOSE STUDY

1 Shanks pretends to admire the statesman. What does he really think?

2 Whose is the 'faint and distant voice'?

3 What does it say about the war dead and the survivors?

4 What is the grim joke in the last verse?

WRITING

Imagine a conversation between the statesman and the ex-soldier on the dole. Base it on the ideas from the poem. The statesman explains the necessity of war, the great sacrifice it has involved and the promise of a better future. The ex-soldier describes the cruel realities of his situation and his bitterness about the loss of so many comrades.

ARMISTICE DAY 1921

The hush begins. Nothing is heard
Save the arrested taxi's throbbing
And here and there an ignorant bird
And here a sentimental woman sobbing.

The statesman bares and bows his head
Before the solemn monument;
His lips, paying duty to the dead
In silence, are more than ever eloquent.

But ere[1] the sacred silence breaks
And taxis hurry on again,
A faint and distant voice awakes,
Speaking the mind of a million absent men:

'Mourn not for us. Our better luck
At least has given us peace and rest.
We struggled when our moment struck
But now we understand that death knew best.

'Would we be as our brothers are
Whose barrel-organs charm the town?
Our was a better dodge by far –
We got *our* pensions in a lump sum down.

'We, out of all, have had our pay.
There is no poverty where we lie:
The graveyard has no quarter day,
The space is narrow but the rent not high.

'No empty stomach here is found;
Unless some cheated worm complain
You hear no grumbling underground:
O, never, never wish us back again!

'Mourn not for us, but rather we
Will meet upon this solemn day
And in our greater liberty
Keep silent for you, a little while, and pray.'

EDWARD SHANKS

[1] **ere:** *before*

Survivors were haunted by their battle experiences for years. Modern psychologists recognize this state of delayed shock in war veterans, but in 1918 men were left to manage as best they could. An Australian, Vance Palmer, served in France. He imagines a man who cannot forget the war, even when he returns, apparently unhurt, to his farm in the Australian bush.

THE FARMER REMEMBERS THE SOMME

Will they never fade or pass –
The mud, and the misty figures endlessly coming
In file through the foul morass,
And the grey flood-water lipping the reeds and grass,
And the steel wings drumming?

The hills are bright in the sun:
There's nothing changed or marred in the well-known
   places;
When work for the day is done
There's talk, and quiet laughter, and gleams of fun
On the old folks' faces.

I have returned to these;
The farm, and kindly Bush[1] and the young calves
   lowing;
But all that my mind sees
Is a quaking bog in a mist – stark, snapped trees,
And the dark Somme flowing.

VANCE PALMER

[1] **Bush:** *Australian countryside*

CLOSE STUDY

Palmer sets two landscapes, of war and peace, beside each other.

1   How does one represent life and the other death?

2   Which key words create the **mood** of each?

3   Comment on the **structure** of the poem and the effect of **juxtaposing** the present reality with his memories of the Somme.

WRITING

Then and now: an old serviceman or woman looks back on war after his or her return to ordinary life. Write their recollections and experiences in the form of a first person narrative. Consider:

• What are they doing now the war is over?
• What sights or situations give rise to their memories of the war?

• What dangers, sounds and sights come back to them and how do they feel about these now?
• What do they remember about their old comrades or friends?
• What do they value about their present life?

Sad journeys by relatives to the old Western Front battlefields were a feature of the post-war years. Violet Markham described such a visit in 1919.

> The surface is a series of shell holes filled with stagnant water, green, disgusting … The trenches run like a crazy quilt in every direction … Silence as though gods and men alike had shrunk back appalled at the spectacle of the mangled earth …

The Nineteenth century 1919

Geoffrey Fyson returned to Vimy Ridge near Arras, where he fought in the costly advance of April 1917. To him, this was a haunted place where many friends died. He resented the coach loads of tourists who disturbed this precious ground.

VIMY RIDGE

From Arras, on the straight white road
   Where all marched up, where some limped back,
Now, motor-load on motor-load,
   The tourists mass for the attack.

Over each splintered track we trod,
   Over each shelving trench we made,
Over each grass-grown space – Ah, God! –
   Where dust of my friends in dust is laid,

Cheerful, loud-voiced battalions pass,
   Gorging the sights their money buys …
While you are sleeping 'neath the grass,
   You who have waked beyond the skies,

Keep everlasting silence. Yet
   Are glad, maybe, when eve draws on,
When stilled the turmoil is, and fret,
   And Arras chants her carillon,[1]

When round-eyed children with soft tread
   Draw near, and frame a diadem[2]
Of glowing poppies, that are red
   Because your blood has watered them.

GEOFFREY FYSON

[1] **carillon:** *chime of bells*
[2] **diadem:** *a crown or headband*

CLOSE STUDY

1 The white road from Arras brings two scenes to his mind. What are these?

2 What are the dark jokes in 'The tourists mass for the attack' and 'Cheerful, loud-voiced battalions'?

3 Why are the 'splintered track', 'shelving trench' and 'grass grown space' so precious to him?

4 Which words tell us that he hates the tourists? By contrast, how does he imagine his friends?

5 He finds consolation in the evening when the tourists have left. Who provide appropriate remembrance for the dead? How do they do this? Why are the poppies such an effective expression of remembrance?

WRITING

The two minutes' silence is now widely observed on Remembrance Day, 11 November. Here is a description of the silence in London in 1919:

> As I stood there, "sorrow's keenest wind" cut across many memories ... How many are now filling lonely graves on France and Flanders? ... Everything was still. Through the trees the streams of vehicles could be seen halted, and people, people everywhere were standing with bared heads ... One heard hysterical cries and sobs ...

The Times: 12 November 1919

1 Write a poem or short sketch about the thoughts of someone on Remembrance Day 1919, or of yourself in November this year. Try to use contrasts between the present and the past, peace and war, to achieve effects.

2 Perhaps you have visited the old Western Front trenches and memorials on holiday or a school visit. If not, use some of the pictures in this section. Write a poem or short prose sketch about your thoughts in those extraordinary places. Try to mix images (sights, sounds) from the present with images from the past to achieve effects.

War cemetery, Etaples, 1919: John Lavery

POSTSCRIPT TO FIRST WORLD WAR POEMS

This poem, written during the war, is an amazing, and sad, piece of prophecy.

Joseph Leftwich came from a Polish-Jewish family which settled in London. He shared an East End boyhood with Isaac Rosenberg (see pp. 89-92). He fiercely opposed the war, from which, having been born in neutral Holland, he was exempted.

● CLOSE STUDY

1   What is remarkable about this poem's general message?

2   What is uncanny about its details:

    We must fight their sons,
    Or some other one. ...?

3   Why does the writer see war as pointless?

4   Was he right in your opinion?

● DISCUSSION

Compare this poem with this famous 1918 painting by Paul Nash. In what ways are they like and unlike each other?

We are making a new world (detail): Paul Nash

WAR

Over the World
Rages war.
Earth, sea and sky
Wince at his roar.

He tramples down
At every tread,
A million men,
A million dead.

We say that we
Must crush the Hun,[1]
Or else the World
Will be undone.
But Huns are we
As much as they.
All men are Huns,
Who fight and slay.

And if we win,
And crush the Huns,
In twenty years
We must fight their sons,
Who will rise against
Our victory,
Their fathers', their own
Ignominy.[2]

And if their Kaiser[3]
We dethrone,
They will his son restore,
Or some other one.
If we win by war,
War is a force,
And others to war
Will have recourse.

And through the World
Will rage new war.
Earth, sea and sky
Will wince at his roar.
He will trample down
At every tread,
Millions of men,
Millions of dead.

JOSEPH LEFTWICH

[1] **Huns:** *Germans*
[2] **ignominy:** *disgrace*
[3] **Kaiser:** *German Emperor*

PART 3
THE SECOND WORLD WAR
1939-45

Poetry was still a fashion in the Second World War. Memories of Owen and Sassoon made many men and women read and write poetry in the long periods of boredom between the violent episodes of the war. Most of this writing is about experience. There was little of the anger and satire of the First War: it was widely accepted that the struggles against the German Nazis and the Japanese were necessary and just.

Although there were remarkable poems and poets, somehow the poetry of the Second War does not make as great an impact as that of the First. It is the *words* of Wilfred Owen and others that create our mental picture of trench warfare. By 1939 other media – notably photography and film – had begun to replace the written word in making the most vivid and lasting images of the Second World War.

We can only include a few poems here which give us glimpses of people's lives and thoughts.

We only watch, and indicate and make our scribbled pencil notes,
We do not wish to moralize, only to ease our dusty throats.

Donald Bain, from *War Poet*

Battle of Britain, August – October 1940: Paul Nash

UNIT 19 //
Glimpses of war

Vera Brittain was best known for her autobiography *Testament of Youth* (1933), about her nursing experience in the First World War. She became a determined peace campaigner in the 1920s and '30s. She was therefore bitterly disappointed by the renewal of war with Germany on 3 September 1939. That Sunday, she heard Prime Minister Chamberlain's radio broadcast declaration of war, while she was staying at her cottage in the New Forest. She noted in her diary:

*His voice sounded old and trembled ...
I found that tears were running down my
cheeks - from some subconscious realization
of the failure of my efforts for peace over
20 years ... went out into the forest ...
it was impossible to take in the size of
the catastrophe ...*

SEPTEMBER, 1939

The purple asters lift their heads
Beneath the azure[1] autumn skies;
Above the sunflower's golden cup
Hover the scarlet butterflies.

Not in the sandbagged city street
Where London's silver guardians[2] soar,
But through the cottage garden throbs
The aching grief of England's war.

VERA BRITTAIN

[1] **azure:** *blue*
[2] **silver guardians:** *barrage balloons*

◉ CLOSE STUDY

1 What are the beauties of the late summer in the country garden?

2 What changes has war brought to London?

3 Why does the coming of war seem more poignant in the country than in the city?

4 How does the **structure** of the poem help to convey this?

5 Which words sum up Vera Brittain's sorrow at the return of war?

The terrifying air bombing of British cities in the Blitz of 1940–41 meant that whole populations were involved in war. As a result of German air-raids, 60,595 civilians lost their lives.

In a word sketch, E.J. Scovell remembers her feelings as a mother before and after a night-time German air-raid.

DAYS DRAWING IN

The days fail: night broods over afternoon:
And at my child's first drink beyond the night
Her skin is silver in the early light.
Sweet the grey morning and the raiders gone.

E.J. SCOVELL

◉ CLOSE STUDY

1 Which words show the fear and tension of waiting for the German raids?

2 How does the poet show that the child is precious to the mother?

3 Which words express the relief at morning and survival?

Frances Cornford, friend of Rupert Brooke (see p.42) reflects on the strange contrasts of night and morning after a raid.

(see p.42)

AUTUMN BLITZ

Unshaken world! Another day of light
After the human chaos of the night;
Although a heart in mendless horror grieves,
What calmly yellow, gently falling leaves!

FRANCES CORNFORD

◉ CLOSE STUDY

1 What ideas are suggested by the phrase 'chaos of the night'?

2 What is the meaning of 'a heart in mendless horror grieves'?

3 What continues, surprisingly, throughout the bombing attack?

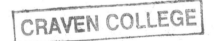
CRAVEN COLLEGE

The Blitz. *A house collapsing on two firemen, Shoe Lane, London*: Leonard Rosoman

Many feared that Hitler would use poison gas bombs, and everyone was issued with a gas mask. W.H. Davies, the celebrated 'tramp poet' of the pre-1914 era, was horrified that children, even babies, had to wear such masks.

ARMED FOR WAR

Is life on Earth a viler thing
    Than ever was known before?
Who shall we ask – the wise old man
    Whose years have reached five score?

When we have questioned Church and State,
    Is there anyone else to ask?
Is it the Baby, three weeks old,
    That wears a gas-proof mask?

Is it the Infant armed to meet
    A poisoned earth and sky –
A thing too weak to lift its hand
    To rub a sleepy eye?

W.H. DAVIES

⬤ CLOSE STUDY

Having been brought up in what seemed a kinder, simpler Victorian/Edwardian age, Davies feels that the new war is the darkest time in human history.

1 Whom does he imagine consulting about the truth of this idea?

2 What is suggested about his attitude by the series of questions that he asks?

3 What is so poignant about his picture of the baby?

4 Which words describe the threat of the world into which it is born?

The coming of war in 1939 caused great social upheaval in Britain. Fear of air bombing led to mass evacuation of the population from threatened areas. The priority group, school children, was moved from the cities to the countryside in 'Operation Pied Piper', which began on 1 September 1939. Labelled and clutching gas mask boxes, children packed trains and buses and were swept off to vaguely known destinations.

R.S. Thomas, a Welsh clergyman and an outstanding poet, creates an imaginary picture of one such child in his poem below. A small girl of seven or eight has come to a Welsh farm to escape the bombing in the city she left.

THE EVACUEE

She woke up under a loose quilt
Of leaf patterns, woven by the light
At the small window, busy with the boughs
Of a young cherry; but wearily she lay,
Waiting for the siren[1], slow to trust
Nature's deceptive peace, and then afraid
Of the long silence, she would have crept
Uneasily from the bedroom with its frieze
Of fresh sunlight, had not a cock crowed,
Shattering the surface of that limpid[2] pool
Of stillness, and before the ripples died
One by one in the field's shallows,
The farm woke with uninhibited[3] din.

And now the noise and not the silence drew her
Down the bare stairs at great speed.
The sounds and voices were a rough sheet
Waiting to catch her, as though she leaped
From a scorched storey of the charred past.

And there the table and the gallery
Of farm faces trying to be kind
Beckoned her nearer, and she sat down
Under an awning of salt hams.

And so she grew, a small bird in the nest
Of welcome that was built about her,
Home now after so long away
In the flowerless streets of the drab town.
The men watched her busy with the hens,
The soft flesh ripening warm as corn
On the sticks of limbs, the grey eyes clear,
Rinsed with dew of their long dread.
The men watched her, and, nodding, smiled
With earth's charity, patient and strong.

R.S. THOMAS

[1] **siren:** *to mark beginning or end of air-raid*
[2] **limpid:** *clear*
[3] **uninhibited:** *unrestrained*

CLOSE STUDY

Section 1

1   Describe where the girl wakes up after her evacuation journey.

2   What do we learn about the girl's past and its effect on her feelings as she awakes?

3   The section is rich in **imagery** that sets the scene and suggests the **atmosphere**. Select examples and comment on how Thomas uses them.

4   What **comparison** is used to describe the cock crow that wakes the farm?

Sections 2 and 3

5   Explain the **metaphor** of the 'rough sheet'.

6   How do these stanzas build on the picture of the farm created in the first stanza?

Section 4

Time passes and the girl grows stronger and happier in her new environment.

7   Examine the **similes** and **metaphors** used to describe the changes in the girl. What links all of them? Comment on why the **images** are appropriate.

8   Why is the girl 'home now' when she has been evacuated from her home in the city?

There is a major **theme** in this poem: city living distorts human beings creating the conditions that produce wars, while country living is closely related to nature, love and kindness.

9   Look through the poem and list words and phrases that suggest that city life is ugly and destructive (include war damage). Then list the contrasting words and phrases that praise and value country living.

10   Do you agree with the poet's theme?

WRITING

1   Imagine that in middle age, long after the war, the girl in the poem writes an account of her experience for her grandchildren. Write her story, including her memories of the bombings, her arrival at the Welsh farm, her first morning there and her life over later months.

Take incidents and ideas from the poem but add others from your imagination. Try to structure your piece imaginatively, cutting between her countryside experience and her life in the city.

2   Look at this drawing of evacuees, each labelled and holding a gas mask, preparing to leave London. Write your own evacuation story about one or several of the children.

Consider:
*   Whom are they leaving behind and how long do they expect it to be for?
*   Describe the scene at the station – the noises, sights and feelings of the children and parents.
*   Describe their thoughts as they travel through unfamiliar country.
*   What is their new home like and what do they like and dislike about it?

The evacuation of children from Southend, 2 June 1940: Ethel Gabain

While British civilians suffered bombing, RAF Bomber Command struck back at Germany. Eventually massive fleets of bombers, sometimes a thousand strong, devastated German cities. The campaign was costly: nearly 7000 bombers were shot down, and 55,573 flight crew perished. Men of enormous courage and skill, they were celebrated in this poem by the famous playwright and screen-writer Noel Coward.

LIE IN THE DARK AND LISTEN

Lie in the dark and listen,
It's clear tonight so they're flying high
Hundreds of them, thousands perhaps,
Riding the icy, moonlight sky.
Men, materials, bombs and maps
Altimeters and guns and charts
Coffee, sandwiches, fleece-lined boots
Bones and muscles and minds and hearts
English saplings with English roots
Deep in the earth they've left below
Lie in the dark and let them go
Lie in the dark and listen.

Lie in the dark and listen
They're going over in waves and waves
High above villages, hills and streams
Country churches and little graves
And little citizen's worried dreams.
Very soon they'll have reached the sea
And far below them will lie the bays
And coves and sands where they used to be
Taken for summer holidays.
Lie in the dark and let them go
Lie in the dark and listen.

Lie in the dark and listen
City magnates and steel contractors,
Factory workers and politicians
Soft, hysterical little actors
Ballet dancers, 'Reserved'[1] musicians,
Safe in your warm, civilian beds.
Count your profits and count your sheep
Life is flying above your heads
Just turn over and try to sleep.
Lie in the dark and let them go
Theirs is a world you'll never know
Lie in the dark and listen.

NOEL COWARD

[1] **reserved:** *jobs spared from conscription*

⚙ CLOSE STUDY

Civilians lie in their beds and listen to the bombers droning overhead on their way to Germany. Coward imagines what it is like inside the aircraft, and lists some of their contents.

1   What does he value most among these 'items'?

2   Comment on the **metaphor** used to describe the airmen and what it suggests about their age.

3   The second stanza describes the English landscape that the bombers cross. Why does he say 'little graves' and 'little citizen'?

4   What do the features of the landscape tell us about the airmen and their purpose in flying?

5   In the third stanza, he pictures civilians in their beds. Which words and phrases show his contempt for their comforts that contrast with the discomfort and courage of the fliers?

6   What does 'Theirs is a world you'll never know' mean?

7   What is the meaning and force of the repeated line 'Lie in the dark and listen'? How does the **rhyme scheme** add emphasis to this line?

A bomber crew gets ready to fly: *Take off*: Laura Knight

Soldiers of 1939–45 fought on battlegrounds across the world: in the desert of Libya, in the jungles of Burma, on Pacific islands, on Normandy beaches, on Greek islands. Aircraft and tanks made battles more open and rapidly moving, and so prevented too many stagnant trench war situations from developing. There may have been less anger about poor leadership, but the pity of war, in its effects on the individual, remained the key theme of soldiers' poetry and prose-writing.

Keith Douglas, artist and poet, is often thought of as the Wilfred Owen of the Second World War. Called up from Oxford University where he was studying, he became a tank commander and, in 1942, fought at El Alamein, the decisive British victory over the Germans in the Libyan desert of North Africa. On 6 June 1944, he took part in the D-Day landings in Normany, but was killed by a shell splinter three days later.

In his prose description *Alamein to Zem Zem*, Douglas recalled 'the violent impressions … the black and bright incidents of battle'. He was fascinated by what he saw:

> It is exciting and amazing to see thousands of men … having to kill and be killed, and yet at intervals moved by a feeling of comradeship with the men who kill them and whom they kill.

He also wrote about what he had seen in bold and striking poems. *Vergissmeinnicht* is one of these, composed at an army base in 'a hole in the sand'.

VERGISSMEINNICHT[1]

Three weeks gone and the combatants gone
returning over the nightmare ground
we found the place again, and found
the soldier sprawling in the sun.

The frowning barrel of his gun
overshadowing. As we came on
that day, he hit my tank with one
like the entry of a demon.

Look. Here in the gunpit spoil
the dishonoured picture of his girl
who has put: *Steffi. Vergissmeinnicht*
in a copybook gothic script.

We see him almost with content,
abased, and seeming to have paid
and mocked at by his own equipment
that's hard and good when he's decayed.

But she would weep to see today
how on his skin the swart[2] flies move;
the dust upon the paper eye
and the burst stomach like a cave.

For here the lover and killer are mingled
who had one body and one heart.
and death who had the soldier singled
has done the lover mortal hurt.

KEITH DOUGLAS

[1] **Vergissmeinnicht:** *do not forget me*
[2] **swart:** *dark*

Dead German on the Hitler line, Italy: Charles Comfort

1 What events are described in the first three stanzas?

2 The German anti-tank shot is compared to 'the entry of a demon'. What exactly does this **simile** mean?

3 In stanza 4, what do Douglas and the tank crew feel as they stare at the dead man?

4 How do the photograph and its message alter their feelings about their enemy?

5 What **comparisons** are used to make the description of the dead soldier vivid?

6 In the last stanza, Douglas sums up what he now feels. For him and his men, the German is a killer; for Steffi, the German girl, he is a lover. What does Douglas wish might have happened?

7 What are his final feelings about his enemy?

WRITING

1 Write about the poem
   - What happened before the poem's story starts?
   - What do the tank crew see in the German gun-pit?
   - How do they feel about their enemy?
   - How are their feelings changed by the photograph?
   - What does this poem tell us about 'the pity of war'?

2 In a letter to a close officer friend, Douglas describes this battle incident. Make clear his changing thoughts about the dead German.

Vernon Scannell served in the army in the North African desert and in Normandy from 1941 to 1944. He has described the horror of his battle experiences in many moving poems.

In *Route March Rest*, he shows a group of soldiers marching through the English countryside on a hot day before they embark for the D-Day invasion of France in June 1944. As they look at the English spring in the lanes, and as they rest in a village, they have time to reflect on life – before they face death.

ROUTE MARCH REST

They march in staggered columns through the lanes
Drowsy with dust and summer, rifles slung.
All other-ranks wore helmets and the sun
Drummed on bobbing metal plates and purred
Inside their skulls; the thumping tramp of boots
On gravel crunched. B Company had become
A long machine that clanked and throbbed. The reek
Of leather, sweat and rifle-oil was thick
And khaki on the body of the day.
All dainty fragrances were shouldered out
Though thrush and blackbird song could not be stilled
And teased some favoured regions of the air.

They reached a village and the order came
To halt and fall out for a rest. The men
Unslung their rifles, lit up cigarettes,
And sprawled or squatted on the village green.
Opposite the green, next to the church,
The school, whose open windows with wild flowers
In glass jars on the sills framed pools of dark,
Was silent, cool; but from the playground sprayed
The calls of children, bright as buttercups,
Until a handbell called them in from play
And then B Company was ordered back
To fall in on the road in their platoons
And start the march again.
               Beyond the church
They passed a marble plinth and saw the roll
Of names, too many surely for this small
Community, and as the files trudged on,
Faintly from the school, like breath of flowers
But half-remembered, children's voices rose:
'All things bright and beautiful,' they sang,
Frail sound, already fading, soon to die.

VERNON SCANNELL

CLOSE STUDY

Section 1

1 The helmeted men, marching in full kit, are anonymous. Comment on the **metaphor** used to describe the column of men.

2 Scannell makes you identify with and share the discomforts of the soldiers by strong use of **sensory details**. What ugly military things do the men feel, hear and smell as they march through the lanes?

3 Find words and phrases that suggest their discomfort.

Section 2

4 They fall out to rest on a village green and, for a short time, become individuals. Which details of the village school sound attractive and make a striking contrast with the soldiers' present lives?

5 Why is 'bright as buttercups' a good way of describing the children here?

6 How do the soldiers feel about the children in the village?

Section 3

7 They pass a 'marble plinth', the village war memorial from the Great War of 1914-18. What surprises them about it?

8 What unpleasant thoughts might they have about it?

9 How are the children's voices related to the spring countryside?

10 What sad points about soldiers are made in the last two lines?

WRITING

Imagine that you are one of the soldiers. Write a descriptive account of your observations and thoughts on the march, and of your rest and departure from the village.

COMPARING POEMS

Look back at Wilfred Owen's *Spring Offensive* (p.58). Both poems consider life and death in war. Compare

• their pictures of military life and death
• their use of contrasts from the natural world

Which poem is more impressive?

Troops on the march, 1944: Alex Colville

Like the soldiers in Steven Spielberg's film *Band of Brothers*, Louis Simpson fought with the American Army at the Normandy landings of 1944 and in the advance across Europe afterwards. He recorded key moments in striking poems. Here he writes about an incident in the Ardennes, scene of a heavy German counter-attack during the winter of 1944–45.

THE BATTLE

Helmet and rifle, pack and overcoat
Marched through a forest. Somewhere up ahead
Guns thudded. Like the circle of a throat
The night on every side was turning red.

They halted and they dug. They sank like moles
Into the clammy earth between the trees.
And soon the sentries, standing in their holes,
Felt the first snow. Their feet began to freeze.

At dawn the first shell landed with a crack.
Then shells and bullets swept the icy woods.
This lasted many days. The snow was black.
The corpses stiffened in their scarlet hoods.

Most clearly of that battle I remember
The tiredness in eyes, how hands looked thin
Around a cigarette, and the bright ember
Would pulse with all the life there was within.

LOUIS SIMPSON

● CLOSE STUDY

1   Why does the poet not mention a person in the first two lines, only the things that a person carries?

2   What **comparison** is used to describe the battle line as the men approach it?

3   What are the worst aspects of this winter war?

4   The scene is black and white. What provides the only colour?

5   The last stanza mentions an individual soldier. What is pathetic about him?

6   What does the glowing cigarette seem to represent in the last two lines?

The triumph of the final Allied advance into Germany in April 1945 was darkened by the discovery of the Nazi concentration camps. On 15 April, British troops entered Bergen-Belsen, a camp in northern Germany. 30,000 prisoners barely survived among huge piles of corpses, dead from typhus and starvation. The bodies were buried in vast pits: among them was 15 year old Anne Frank.

Phillip Whitfield, a doctor in the Royal Army Medical Corps, was moved to write this poem about what he had seen.

DAY OF LIBERATION, BERGEN-BELSEN, MAY 1945

We build our own prison walls
but that day the doors fell open,
it was holiday time
in the death camp.

Lift him with courtesy,
this silent survivor.
Battle-dress doctors,
we took him from the truck
and put him to bed.

The moving skeleton
had crippled hands,
his skinny palms held secrets:
when I undid the joints I found
five wheat grains huddled there.
In the faces of other people
I witness my distress.

I close my eyes:
ten thousand wasted people
still piled in the flesh-pits.
Death of one is the death of all.
It is not the dead I pity.

PHILLIP WHITFIELD

CLOSE STUDY

1 What grim joke is there in the first **stanza**?

The 65,000 dead or dying people in Belsen defy our imagination. Whitfield chooses one victim upon whom to concentrate pity and horror.

2 Which two moving **phrases** describe this victim?

3 What does this story about the victim tell us about the camp, and why is it so pitiful?

4 This experience haunts the writer. What is his final reflection on the tragedy of Belsen?

Look over all of these poems about the Second World War.

DISCUSSION

Discuss whether or not they are as impressive and interesting as those of the First War. Give careful reasons for your argument.

WRITING

Write about some or all of the poems.

• What do they tell us about life, about the thoughts and feeling of civilians and soldiers?

• What do you find moving, strange, or interesting about their content and about the way in which they are written?

Bodies in a grave, Belsen: Alex Colville

UNIT 20 //
The shadow of the bomb

A new kind of war began on 6 August 1945, when the Americans exploded an atomic bomb over Hiroshima in Japan.

Having been developed in secret by American and British scientific teams, it was rushed into action under American President Harry Truman who feared the human cost of an invasion of Japan and wished the war to end quickly.

At 8.15 am the bomb was dropped, floating down by parachute until it exploded 2000 feet above the city centre. The aircraft commander saw a 'bright light', then a 'rolling and boiling cloud' with a 'fiery red core'. Survivors on the ground remembered the 'blinding, intense light'. At the epicentre of the explosion, heat incinerated people so completely that only their shadows remained, burned grotesquely into pavements or walls. Blast reduced everything to rubble. Fire destroyed what remained. Some 200,000 people died, some instantly, others after years of 'radiation sickness'. Two days later a second bomb destroyed Nagasaki with 'a giant pillar of purple fire'. The Japanese surrendered. The nuclear age had begun.

The American poet William Stafford imagines a scene in the New Mexico desert just before the test explosion of the first atomic bomb in July 1945. A lizard seems to sense the future extinction of human life on earth that may result from experiments with the mighty destructive power of nuclear energy.

Hiroshima after the Bomb, August 1945

AT THE BOMB TESTING SITE

At noon in the desert a panting lizard
waited for history, its elbows tense,
watching the curve of a particular road
as if something might happen.

It was looking at something farther off
than people could see, an important scene
acted in stone for little selves
at the flute end of consequences.

There was just a continent without much on it
under a sky that never cared less.
Ready for a change, the elbows waited.
The hands gripped hard on the desert.

WILLIAM STAFFORD

[1] **flute:** *narrow channel*

● CLOSE STUDY

1   Why is the lizard 'waiting for history'?

2   The lizard seems stronger and more intelligent
    than the human race, the 'little selves'. What
    does it seem to see that we cannot?

3   What does 'the flute end of consequences'
    mean?

4   Why mention 'a continent without much on it'
    and 'a sky that never cared less'?

5   What is the coming 'change'?

The gigantic power of a nuclear explosion

Millen Brand is an American novelist, poet and
screen-writer. He published this poem thirty years
after Hiroshima in 1975. He imagines two ordinary
civilians just before the explosion of the bomb: Fred
Braun is enjoying a sleepy August afternoon in the
USA while, at the same moment, an anonymous
Japanese is waking to a fine morning in Hiroshima.
The two are linked by the deadly image of the
American bomber releasing its atomic bomb over
the Japanese city.

AUGUST 6, 1945

Fred Braun has just leaned out on a low windowsill
that needs painting. There are cracks in it,
but so far they have let no rain through.
They can wait a little longer.
This moment is his to enjoy,
looking at his apple orchard and two small plum trees
and under them a red napkin of bee balm[1].
It is beautiful and peaceful. His wife
is troweling a flower bed
along the house wall. He hears
the thud of an apple falling, part
of the nice lethargy[2] of the day. And today
across the world
behind a plane, the Enola Gay[3], there floats in the air,
    slowly descending,
a hardly visible thin tube
with a small fuse at one end
that will fire one of two parts at the other end
and explode this almost unnoticeable filament
with a light brighter than the sun. Below,
in the wooden city of Hiroshima
can it not be that a man
has just rolled back one of his living-room shutters
and is looking out on his garden, thinking,
The morning glories[1] on their bamboo sticks,
the blue sky,
how beautiful everything is! Let me enjoy it.
I should be painting shutters,
but they can wait.
The rain does not yet come through.

MILLEN BRAND

[1] **bee balm/morning glories:** *flowers*
[2] **lethargy:** *laziness*
[3] **Enola Gay:** *the B29 bomber from which the atom bomb
    was dropped*

1 What pleasant details do we hear of Braun's home and garden?

2 Why, perhaps, is the **phrase** 'the thud of an apple falling' full of significance?

3 What does 'the nice lethargy of the day' make him postpone?

Now look at the description of the bomb falling on its parachute.

4 What contrasting words and phrases are used to convey its size and its power?

We move to the Japanese in Hiroshima.

5 What does he see and enjoy as he looks out of his window in the early morning?

6 How is he linked to the American? What does he think about the war?

7 How are the last three lines **ironic**?

8 What does this poem tell us about ordinary human beings and war?

The 'Cold War' confrontation of the Super Powers, the USA and the Soviet Union, began after 1945. Spies soon passed details of the atomic bomb to the Russians who developed their own weapons. Until the reunification of Germany in 1990 effectively ended the 'Cold War', peace was maintained by mutual terror of nuclear weapons which both sides possessed in large numbers.

Many writers, poets and film-makers speculated about what it would be like if a nuclear war started. Among them was Edwin Muir, who, in 1948, wrote indirectly about such a conflict in *The Horses*, which the poet T.S. Eliot called 'that great, that terrifying poem of the atomic age'. Muir imagines a final war which causes the collapse of machine-dominated civilization. He sets his poem on a Scottish island, remote enough from the fighting for people to survive.

THE HORSES

Barely a twelvemonth after
The seven days' war that put the world to sleep,
Late in the evening the strange horses came.
By then we had made our covenant[1] with silence,
But in the first few days it was so still
We listened to our breathing and were afraid.
On the second day
The radios failed; we turned the knobs; no answer.
On the third day a warship passed us, heading north,
Dead bodies piled on the deck. On the sixth day
A plane plunged over us into the sea. Thereafter
Nothing. The radios dumb;
And still they stand in corners of our kitchens,
And stand, perhaps, turned on, in a million rooms
All over the world. But now if they should speak,
If on a sudden they should speak again,
If on the stroke of noon a voice should speak,
We would not listen, we would not let it bring
That old bad world that swallowed its children quick[2]
At one great gulp. We would not have it again.
Sometimes we think of the nations lying asleep,
Curled blindly in impenetrable sorrow,
And then the thought confounds us with its
    strangeness.
The tractors lie about our fields; at evening
They look like dank sea-monsters couched and
    waiting.
We leave them where they are and let them rust:
'They'll moulder away and be like other loam[3].'
We make our oxen drag our rusty ploughs,
Long laid aside. We have gone back

Far past our fathers' land.
                And then, that evening
Late in the summer the strange horses came.
We heard a distant tapping on the road,
A deepening drumming; it stopped, went on again
And at the corner changed to hollow thunder.
We saw the heads
Like a wild wave charging and were afraid.
We had sold our horses in our fathers' time
To buy new tractors. Now they were strange to us
As fabulous steeds set on an ancient shield
Or illustrations in a book of knights.
We did not dare go near them. Yet they waited,
Stubborn and shy, as if they had been sent
By an old command to find our whereabouts
And that long-lost archaic[4] companionship.
In the first moment we had never a thought
That they were creatures to be owned and used.
Among them were some half-a-dozen colts
Dropped in some wilderness of the broken world,
Yet new as if they had come from their own Eden.
Since then they have pulled our ploughs and borne our
    loads,
But that free servitude still can pierce our hearts.
Our life is changed; their coming our beginning.

EDWIN MUIR

[1] **covenant:** *agreement*
[2] **quick:** *alive*
[3] **loam:** *soil*
[4] **archaic:** *old-fashioned*

CLOSE STUDY

Section 1: 'Barely … our fathers' land'

1 'The seven days war' reminds us of God's creation of the world in that time, as told in the Book of Genesis. Now He destroys it in seven days. Why is God angry with Man?

2 What, exactly, do the islanders notice about the effects of the fighting?

3 How have the islanders been changed by the war?

4 What **comparison** is used to describe the now dead countries of the world?

5 Explain 'far past our fathers' land'.

Section 2: 'And then … their coming our beginning'

When the 'strange horses' mysteriously arrive on the island, the poem becomes more fantastic and **visionary**. The sound of the horses announces their arrival.

6 List the words and phrases that define these sounds.

7 What other **comparisons** are used to suggest the power and strangeness of the horses?

8 How do the people feel about the horses?

9 What is the 'long lost archaic companionship'?

10 Why have the horses been sent? Who has sent them?

11 Why mention 'Eden'? And the 'colts'?

12 What is the message of the last line? How and why has human life changed?

Think about the **technique** of the poem. Muir uses a flexible **blank verse**. He is very good on **pauses** to underline certain effects.

13 Look again at Section 1. How do the **line-end full stops** and **short sentences** help to create the effect of silence in the post-war world?

14 Pick out the **metaphors** and **similes** in the poem, and discuss their effectiveness.

15 Discuss the **extended metaphor** of the horses themselves. What do they mean and why are they important to the **theme** of the poem?

WRITING

1 Muir wrote several other poems about imaginary wars. Write your own poem or imaginative story about such a final war. If you wish, use Muir's titles below as a starter.

The last war

After a hypothetical war

The day before the last day

2 Imagine you are one of the islanders in the poem. Write about your experiences during and after the war, as diary entries or as a short story. Include the arrival of the horses. Your writing should try to make clear the meaning of the horses as they help to build a better, simpler civilization.

Beach girl: nuclear victim, a fibre-glass sculpture: Colin Self

Roger McGough became famous as one of the 'Liverpool poets' of the 1960s. He uses a jocular, witty, surprising **style** in poems that creates ideas that are apparently amusing but are sometimes tragic in meaning.

A meteorite, landing on the American East Coast, is seen on military radar and mistaken for a Russian missile. An American General orders a massive response and World War Three begins. McGough offers comic and horrific glimpses of the chaos that follows. The black comedy fits the subject: to McGough, the very idea of nuclear war is farcical and futile.

● CLOSE STUDY

(Note: In Greek myth, Icarus flew too near the sun which melted his feather and wax wings. This is a **metaphor** for man's misuse of science. It is used here to show that nuclear weapons are too ingenious and may cause man's destruction.)

1 Why does the General want to start a war?

2 There is a desperate grim humour about the scenes which follow the explosion of the bombs. Which is the most surprising and effective of these?

3 Are there any serious lines here? Which are they?

4 What points does he make about rich and poor?

5 How does he support CND (Campaign for Nuclear Disarmament)?

6 Why is there an extra long line at the end?

7 Would you say that this is a good way to write about nuclear war? Give reasons for your answers.

✎ WRITING

Write your own poem about nuclear war.
Think of everything that you love that would be destroyed by it:

family home countryside cities wild life natural beauty.

□ COMPARING POEMS

The poets in this section write in very different ways about the great issue of nuclear war. Compare the poems, discussing their

* subject matter
* style
* diction
* imagery
* form

Which do you think is most effective?

ICARUS ALLSORTS[1]

'A meteorite is reported to have landed in New England. No damage is said …'

A littlebit of heaven fell
From out the sky one day
It landed in the ocean
Not so very far away
The General at the radar screen
Rubbed his hands with glee
And grinning pressed the button
That started World War Three.

From every corner of the earth
Bombs began to fly
There were even missile jams
No traffic lights in the sky
In the time it takes to blow your nose
The people fell, the mushrooms[2] rose

'House!' cried the fatlady
As the bingohall moved to various parts of the town

'Raus!'[3] cried the German butcher
as his shop came tumbling down

Philip was in the countinghouse
Counting out his money
The Queen was in the parlour
Eating bread and honey

When through the window
Flew a bomb
And made them go all funny

In the time it takes to draw a breath
Or eat a toadstool, instant death

The rich
Huddled outside the doors of their fallout shelters
Like drunken carolsingers

The poor
Clutching shattered televisions
And last week's editions of T.V. Times
(but the very last)

Civil defence volunteers
With their tin hats in one hand
And their heads in the other

C.N.D. supporters
Their ban the bomb badges beginning to rust
Have scrawled 'I told you so' in the dust.

A littlebit of heaven fell
From out the sky one day
It landed in Vermont
North-Eastern U.S.A.
The general at the radar screen
He should have got the sack
But that wouldn't bring
Three thousand million, seven hundred, and sixty-
    eight people back,
Would it?

ROGER McGOUGH

---

[1] **Icarus allsorts:** *a pun on liquorice allsorts, a sweet*
[2] **mushrooms:** *mushroom-shaped clouds from nuclear explosions*
[3] **Raus:** *get out!*

PART 4
NO END TO WAR 1964-2003

In September 1914, the famous writer H.G. Wells proclaimed that the new European conflict was 'the war to end war'. Many front-line soldiers endured the misery of the trenches with this hope: that their lives were buying permanent peace for future generations. This optimism faded after 1918. One of Thomas Hardy's last poems, published just after his death in 1928, reflected this.

Hardy's dark vision was accurate: war has continued relentlessly, sometimes on a massive world scale, sometimes obscurely; sometimes with the latest high-tech weapons, sometimes with machetes, suicide bomb jackets, or guns carried by boys.

> We are getting to the end of visioning
> … that our race may mend by reasoning
> … that when nations set them to lay waste
> Their neighbours' heritage…
> And hack their pleasant plains in festering seams,
> They may again…
> … tickled mad by some demonic force.
>
> *THOMAS HARDY*

American troops landing in Vietnam

Goran Simic, a Bosnian Serb poet with a Muslim wife, endured the three year siege of Sarajevo before escaping to a new life in Canada. He portrays the deadly atmosphere of life in the besieged city.

1   How are ordinary city things – newspapers, crossing a bridge – strangely and horribly changed by the siege?

2   Pity, in this harsh world, seems numbed. How is this shown in two details of what he observes around him?

3   The killing and 'ethnic cleansing' destroy whole families. How is this vast tragedy considered in small details in the poem?

4   How is the hopelessness of the besieged people described in the last stanza?

Obscure, chaotic civil wars still darken life in parts of central Africa. Rwanda became an independent republic in 1962. Its population includes two rival tribal peoples: the Hutu and the Tutsi. Years of ethnic rivalry and violence between them reached a climax in 1994 after the Hutu Rwandan President was killed when his aircraft was shot down. Extremist militias encouraged Hutus, including women and children, to start a systematic massacre of their Tutsi neighbours.

In just 100 frenzied days, 800,000 Tutsis were brutally killed with guns, grenades, machetes, nail-studded clubs and spears. Crazed crowds hunted their victims into schools, churches, even hospitals to finish them off. Victims were hastily buried, while the ring-leaders fled the country. Attempts to stabilize the country and to bring these leaders to justice are still continuing. Alan Jenkins reflects sombrely on this savage and primitive ethnic war.

NEIGHBOURS

When the rains come in Rwanda in a Tutsi village
and the topsoil's washed away, strange shoots
of fingers, toes, knees and elbows, jawbones,

push up from such wrong, unlikely roots
as have lain there since they were slaughtered –
the cowherd and the teacher and the sawbones[1]

and their women and their children and their neighbours
(for unless you are a hermit in a mountain cavern
or a guru[2] in a temple in the jungle, neighbours

are what you naturally, inevitably have,
to share your sunsets and the fruits of your labours),
all waiting quietly now for when they are watered,

when the rains come, in Rwanda, in a Tutsi village.

ALAN JENKINS

[1] **sawbones:** *doctor or surgeon*
[2] **guru:** *spiritual teacher*

1   Heavy seasonal rains usually produce the shoots of new crops. What dreadfully different 'crops' will be revealed this year?

2   What will the 'roots' produce in the future?

3   Why does the poet list 'cowherd, teacher and sawbones'?

4   In an angry bracketed outburst, the poet introduces his **theme** of neighbours. What point is the poet making here?

5   The last line repeats the first. How do the commas alter its meaning?

British soldiers in southern Iraq, April 2003

The declared aim of the controversial Anglo-Australian-American invasion of Iraq in March–April 2003 was to eliminate weapons of mass destruction supposedly held by the Iraqis. A second unspoken aim was simply 'regime change': the removal of the cruel and threatening dictatorship of Saddam Hussein.

Before the war, Andrew Motion, the Poet Laureate, felt, like many people, 'violently opposed' to the invasion. This poem, written after the campaign began, softens anger into **elegy**. As ancient Mesopotamia, Iraq was the cradle of human civilization. Here supposedly, was the mythical Garden of Eden. The first cities, on the banks of the twin rivers, Tigris and Euphrates, produced great art and culture. War, says Andrew Motion, now threatens these great places, real and mythical, and degrades the human race itself.

REGIME CHANGE

Advancing down the road from Nineveh
Death paused a while and said 'Now listen here.

You see the names of places roundabout?
They're mine now, and I've turned them inside out.

Take Eden, further south: At dawn today
I've ordered my troops to tear away

Its walls and gates so everyone can see
That gorgeous fruit which dangles from its tree.

You want it, don't you? Go and eat it then,
And lick your lips, and pick the same again.

Take Tigris and Euphrates; once they ran
Through childhood-coloured slats of sand and sun.

Not any more they don't; I've filled them up
With countless different kinds of human crap.

Take Babylon, the palace sprouting flowers
Which sweetened empires in their peaceful hours –

I've found a different way to scent the air:
Already it's a by-word for despair.

Which leaves Baghdad – the star-tipped minarets,
The marble courts and halls, the mirage-heat.

These places, and the ancient things you know,
You won't know soon. I'm working on it now.'

ANDREW MOTION

[1] **Nineveh:** *ancient city on the Tigris*
[2] **fruit:** *forbidden fruit from the Tree of Knowledge*
[3] **Babylon:** *ancient city on the Euphrates*

● CLOSE STUDY

1   Death (or the Devil) talks in contrasting styles.
    • Where does he speak crudely?
    • Where does he speak poetically of the beauties of ancient Iraq?

2   The ancient places will be 'turned inside out'. Which words and **phrases** tell you of the changes to the
    • twin rivers
    • ancient Babylon
    • Baghdad?

3   How does the poet use the Biblical Garden of Eden myth in this protest against war?

4   Do you like the rough **rhymed couplets**? Where are they most effective?

5   Now that you have read the poem, what two meanings can you see in its title?

✐ WRITING

Think about scenes from recent wars that you have seen on television news. Write your own angry or **elegiac** poem about some of the people involved and the effects of war upon them.

● COMPARING POEMS

Read over these four poems about recent wars. Then choose *two* that impress you. Compare them with *two* other poems from the First, or from the Second, World War.

Consider:

•   subject matter
•   theme
•   form
•   diction
•   imagery

Which do you prefer? Make your reasons clear.

APPENDICES

Questions for Further Study

TOPICS FOR WRITTEN WORK

PRE-1914 WAR POEMS

? FOUNDATION QUESTIONS

1 Choose two poems you have studied that show the horror of war most forcefully. Say:

- what happens in each poem;
- how the poets use language to make their points.

2 Choose two poems which show contrasting pictures of:

- the glamour and excitement;
- the suffering of war.

Say what happens in each and point out some ways in which the poets use language to make their points.

3 Choose two poems in which women are involved. Write about the poems, showing the effect that war has on women.

? HIGHER QUESTIONS

1 Choose two of the poems and explore the ways in which the poets show war and its sufferings to us.

2 These poems often tell strong and vivid stories. Choose two that have impressed you and explain the power of the events, commenting on the poets' use of language, structure and form.

3 You have been asked to give a short talk explaining the interest of war poetry written before the First World War. Write the talk, illustrating closely from two poems that have impressed you.

POST-1914 WAR POEMS

? FOUNDATION QUESTIONS

1 Write about two poems where the setting and atmosphere contribute strongly to the ideas expressed by the poets.

2 These poems tell strong and memorable stories about war. Choose two that have impressed you, outline the story of each, and explain how the language of the poems underlines their effect.

3 Which one poem that you have studied shows the misery and horror of modern war most forcibly? Consider the subject matter and the way in which the poem is written.

? HIGHER QUESTIONS

1 Discuss two poems from this section which are angry and bitter about war and its effects. Discuss the ideas and language of each. Which, finally, is more memorable and why?

2 Choose two poems where settings are important. How do the poets use the settings to underline their ideas about modern war?

3 You are asked to write a short introduction to Wilfred Owen or Siegfried Sassoon. Do this using close evidence about style and subject matter from two poems by either poet.

4 Think of two poems in this section which make you feel sympathy for people caught up in war. Describe the people and their situations. Analyse how the poets' style and choice of language create this sympathy. Which poem is more impressive?

CRAVEN COLLEGE

TOPICS FOR SPOKEN ACTIVITY

1 Prepare a short 'programme' for radio (tape recorder) or TV (video recorder) on a set of poems, or a particular poet, that you like. Include expressive readings of the poems and some background.

2 Role play a meeting between two young people with opposed views on war (Jessie Pope and Wilfred Owen would be good examples). Show their ideas on patriotism, duty and sacrifice. Quotes examples from war poetry to support her/his views.

3 Prepare, with a friend, a careful, close reading of a chosen favourite poem. You might read alternate lines or sections. You could add music. Make a recording of your finished product.

4 Which era of war poetry is the best? Look at your chosen era closely and illustrate carefully from several poems when you describe its merits to your friends.

5 Give a talk on a particular poet chosen from those included in the book. Do further research into the poet's life and work. Read and discuss several poems, using those included in this book and others that you find.

6 Choose two similar poems. Give a talk to the class comparing them, showing how they are alike and unlike in subject matter, language and style.

7 Working in a group, prepare an assembly session where you introduce some of the poems you have enjoyed (either from pre- or post-1914). Each person reads a poem with expression and then says something about the poet and the ideas he or she expresses.

8 Which is the best poem in *War Poems*? Make a group with others who also choose their favourite. Each person reads the poem aloud and comments on subject and language, explaining why it should be considered the best.

Into A–Level // Advanced Questions

The questions that follow concentrate largely on the period of the Great War and are intended as practice questions for students looking in depth at this period. The first one includes a suggested essay plan that you will find on the next page.

The aim in any response should be a well constructed argument that makes detailed reference to the poems and in which critical vocabulary is used appropriately.

? QUESTIONS

1 Many poets fighting in, or observing, the First World War voiced criticism of its conduct and its terrible effects. They responded in two ways: sorrow (elegy) and anger (satire).

From the selection of First World War poems in this book, choose and discuss three elegies and three angry, satirical poems. Consider

- language, form and structure
- the writers' thoughts and feelings about war and contemporary society
- the influence of the time of composition
- the gender of the writers.

Compare the two approaches and reach a conclusion about which was more expressive and effective.

Into A–Level continued

POSSIBLE PLAN FOR QUESTION 1:

a) Short introduction about the change from war as a glorious adventure (see introduction to 'Ideals and chivalry') to a nightmare of attrition fighting (see introduction to 'Realities of trench warfare')

b) Elegiac poems:
Choose one important poem (*Spring Offensive* or *Futility* : Owen, or *Dead Man's Dump*: Rosenberg) and two others that you admire (such as *Cannon-fodder*: Waugh; *The Armistice*: Cannan; *The Sniper*: Cocker; *For the Fallen*: Binyon; or *Vimy Ridge*: Fyson).

Write two paragraphs on the major poem, discussing especially

- the writer's thoughts and feelings
- language, form and structure

Write one paragraph each on the other two poems.

c) Angry, satirical poems:
Again, choose an important poem (*Dulce et Decorum est*: Owen; *Suicide in the Trenches* or *The General*: Sassoon; or *The Other Side*: Frankau) and two others (such as *God! How I Hate You*: West; *Manslaughter Morning*: Tomlinson; *Five Souls*: Ewer; *The New Trade*: Golding; or *I Shouted for Blood*: Begbie).

d) Draw the argument together by comparing details of language and theme in <u>two</u> poems (one from 'elegy' and one from 'satire') that impress you.

e) Reach a final conclusion about which style of writing is more impressive and memorable.

? QUESTIONS

2 To some of the poets in this book, war seems a glorious adventure. To others, it is merely brutal, pointless destruction.

Re-read the pre- and post-1914 poems listed below. Write a comparison of the ways in which the poets consider the glory or futility of war.

The Battle of Blenheim: Southey (p.13)
Vitaï Lampada: Newbolt (p.22)
The Soldier: Brooke (p.43)
from *Dulce et Decorum:* Glasgow (p.44)
from *The Other Side:* Frankau (p.51)
Dulce et Decorum est: Owen (p.77)
Dead Man's Dump: Rosenberg (p.90)

3 Look again at

Who's for the game?: Pope (p.38)
The Volunteer: Asquith (p.42)
from *The Other Side:* Frankau (p.51)
from *France 1917:* Wilson (p.54)
Suicide in the Trenches: Sassoon (p.72)
Futility: Owen (p.80)
The Armistice: Cannan (p.94)

Examine how typical in style and treatment of subject matter these poems are in the literature of the First World War. You should consider

- language, form and structure
- the poets' thoughts and feelings about war and contemporary society
- the influence of the time of composition
- the gender of the poets.

In your answer, you may include evidence from your wider reading in the literature of the First World War.

4 In 1936, the poet W.B. Yeats excluded Wilfred Owen from his edition of *The Oxford Book Of Verse* because 'passive suffering is not a theme for poetry'. He further described Owen's poems as 'all blood, dirt and sucked sugar stick'.

Argue against Yeats to show that Wilfred Owen's poems are in fact profound elegies on and protests against twentieth-century warfare. Refer closely to at least <u>four</u> of the poems included in this book.

5 'Where are the war poets?' wrote a critic in 1940, suggesting that the great tradition of war poetry had died out after 1918.

By referring in detail to any <u>four</u> poems in Parts 3 and 4 of this book, show that thoughtful, expressive and moving poetry was still being written in 1939-45, or in later wars.

Further reading

General

The Oxford book of war poetry: ed. Jon Stallworthy, Oxford 1984 (chronological)

The Faber book of war poetry: ed. Kenneth Baker, Faber 1996 (thematic)

War stories: ed. Christopher Martin, Collins Cascades 2001 (non-fiction/fiction to match themes of this book)

War poems: (audio tape) HarperCollins 1997 (contains many of the poems in this book)

The spoken word: poets (CD): The British Library 2003 (Poets reading their own work: Tennyson *(Charge of Light Brigade);* Newbolt *(Vitae Lampada);* Binyon *(For the fallen);* Sassoon *(Attack; Died of wounds)*

Pre-1914 Poetry

Theirs but to do or die: ed. Patrick Waddington, Astra 1995 (Crimean war poems)

The white man's burden: ed. Chris Brooks and Peter Faulkner, University of Exeter Press 1996 (poems of British Empire)

Drummer Hodge: Malvern van Wyk Smith, Oxford 1978 (poems of Boer War)

The First World War

The First World War: Martin Gilbert, HarperCollins 1995

World War I: Simon Adams, Dorling Kindersley 2001

1914–18: Jay Winter and Blaire Baggett, BBC Books (+ videos) 1996

The Great War: BBC (videos) 2002 (famous 1964 TV series)

Forgotten voices of the Great War: Max Arthur, Ebury Press 2002 (letters and diaries)

www.firstworldwar.com (useful general site)

Poetry

Poetry of the Great War: ed. Dominic Hibberd and John Onions, Macmillan 1986

The war poets: ed. Robert Giddings, Bloomsbury 1988

A deep cry: First World War soldier poets: ed. Anne Powell, Sutton 1988

First World War poets: Alan Judd and David Crane, National Portrait Gallery 1997 (excellent portraits and commentary)

Scars upon my heart: ed. Catherine Reilly, Virago 1981 (women's verse)

Anthem for doomed youth: Jon Stallworthy, Constable 2002 (good manuscript material)

Poets of the Great War (audio tape): Naxos 1997

Wilfred Owen

The war poems: ed. Jon Stallworthy, Chatto and Windus 1994

Selected letters: ed. John Bell, Oxford 1985

Wilfred Owen: the last year: Dominic Hibberd, Constable 1992

Wilfred Owen: Dominic Hibberd, Orion 2002 (two outstanding biographies)

Owen the poet: Dominic Hibberd, Macmillan 1986 (excellent commentary on the poems)

www.wilfred.owen.association.mcmail.com (useful virtual tour of places in Owen's life, and wide range of manuscripts)

Siegfried Sassoon

The war poems: ed. Rupert Hart-Davis, Faber 1983

Diaries 1915–18, Faber 1983 (brilliant background to poems)

The complete memoirs of George Sherston, Faber 1972 (semi-fictitious memoirs)

www.geocities.com/CapitolHill/8103/index.html (poems and war paintings)

Fiction / non-fiction prose and drama

Goodbye to all that: Robert Graves (1929), Penguin Modern Classics

Undertones of war: Edmund Blunden (1928), Penguin Modern Classics

The Secret Battle: A.P. Herbert (1919), Oxford University Press (an officer shot at dawn)

Her privates we: Frederic Manning (1930), Penguin Modern Classics

All Quiet on the Western Front: Erich Remarque (1928), Vintage Classics (new translation)

Not so quiet... Stepdaughters of war: Helen Zenna Smith (1930), Virago (a woman ambulance driver)

Testament of Youth: Vera Brittain (1933), Virago

Letters from a lost generation: ed. Alan Bishop and Mark Bostridge, Abacus 1999 (1914–18 letters of Vera Brittain and her friends)

Journey's End: R.C. Sherriff (1929), Penguin Modern Classics (war play)

Further reading continued

Art

A bitter truth: Richard Cork,
Yale University Press 1994

www.art-ww1.com/gb/peintre.html
(100 painters from 1914–18)

www.warmuseum.ca/cwm/canvas/cwint01.html
(Canadian War Museum paintings)

The Second World War

The Second World War: Martin Gilbert,
HarperCollins 1998

World War 2: Simon Adams, Dorling Kindersley 2000

The World at War (videos): ITV

www.iwm.org.uk (Imperial War Museum site)

Poetry

Poetry of the Second World War: ed. Desmond Graham,
Chatto and Windus 1995

The Terrible Rain: the war poets 1939-1945: ed. Brian
Gardner, Methuen 1966

Shadows of War: ed. Anne Powell, Sutton 1999
(women's poetry)

Chaos of the Night: ed. Catherine Reilly, Virago 1984
(women's poetry)

Holocaust Poetry: ed. Hilda Schiff, HarperCollins
(Fount) 1995

Fiction / non-fiction prose

Alamein to Zem-Zem: Keith Douglas (1946),
Penguin Modern Classics (desert war)

Vessel of Sadness: William Woodruff (1969),
Chatto / Dent (Italian Front)

Fleshwounds: David Holbrook (1966),
Methuen (D-Day)

The Diary of Anne Frank (1947),
Longman Imprint edition 1989

Hiroshima: John Hersey (1946),
Penguin Modern Classics

Glossary

abstract idea: an idea, imagined in the mind, that does not actually exist.

adjective: describes or modifies a noun.

archaism (adjective: **archaic**): out-dated word or phrase.

atmosphere: the feeling or mood created in the mind by a place or setting.

ballad: a simple narrative poem. Each four line stanza contains a refrain. It is intended to be sung or chanted.

colloquial: language that sounds like everyday, familiar speech.

comparison: saying that one thing is like another. Poetic imagery is the technical name for this.

couplet: a pair of rhyming lines.

dialogue: conversation between two or more people.

diction: the poet's choice and use of words.

elegy (adjective: **elegiac**): a sad poem or song mourning someone's death.

epic: grand/heroic.

epigram (adjective: **epigrammatic**): a short poem containing a clever or surprising thought. It can be satirical.

euphemism: polite word for something distasteful.

free verse: it does not follow the usual verse forms or meters. Each line is a statement with no regular rhythm. When the statement is finished, whether long or short, a new line begins. It gives the impression of quick, spontaneous thought.

grotesque: very strange or ugly.

half-rhyme (or **para-rhyme**): rhyme with similar consonant but different vowel sounds (cold/called)

imagery: technical word for the various kinds of comparisons made in poems (mostly simile or metaphor).

irony (adjective: **ironic**): the humorous or sarcastic use of words to imply the opposite of what they mean or what is expected.

metaphor: an indirect or suggested comparison.

meter: the way in which verse is arranged in patterns, using stressed or unstressed syllables which make up poetic feet. Different meters have different names which describe the number of feet in the line. e.g. tetrameter (4), pentameter (5) or hexameter (6).

narrative poem: one which tells a story.

octet (or **octave**): the first 8 line section of an Italian sonnet.

onomatopoeia (adjective: **onomatopoeic**): use of words that imitate sounds.

oxymoron: placing together ideas that contradict.

participle: the –ing form of the verb.

pathetic fallacy: where landscapes and objects, that are not alive, are shown as having, or reflecting, human feelings or moods.

personification (verb: **personify**): attributing a personal nature, e.g. a human quality, to a thing or idea.

phrase: a group of words that contains an idea (but not a complete verb) and is part of a sentence.

poet laureate: official poet to the British King or Queen.

refrain: a chorus that is repeated, often at the end of a stanza.

rhyme: words that rhyme end with the same sound. Usually the vowels in rhyming words are the same, and the consonants different (e.g. cold/sold).

rhyme scheme: the pattern of line-ending rhymes in a poem.

rhythm: the beat of a line of poetry.

satirical (noun: **satire**): attacking ideas, people or society by mockery.

setting: the time and place described in a poem.

sestet: the last six line section of an Italian sonnet.

simile: a direct comparison that starts with 'like' or 'as'.

sonnet: a 14 line poem in pentameter rhythm with a rhyme scheme of various patterns. The two most important are Italian (8 + 6) and English (4 + 4 + 4 + 2).

stanza: a verse or group of lines that form a unit.

stress: the syllable given most emphasis in a poetic foot. It is usually marked (/).

style: the way in which a writer expresses an idea.

syllable: a separate sound within a word e.g. 'independent' has 4 syllables.

theme: the general idea developed in a poem.

unstressed: the syllable given less emphasis in a poetic foot. It is usually marked (u).

verb: defines an action or a state (a doing or being word).

verse form: the shape and pattern of lines or stanzas in a poem.

Index of Titles

Index of Poets

Text Acknowledgements

The author and publisher would like to thank the following for permission to reproduce poems. While every effort has been made to contact copyright holders, this has not proved to be possible in every case.

p1   'The Victors' by Wilfrid Gibson, reprinted by permission of Mrs Dorothy Gibson.

p5   'On the Idle Hill of Summer' by A. E. Housman, reprinted by permission of The Society of Authors as the Literary Representative of the Estate of A. E. Housman.

p15   'Before Waterloo, the Last Night' by Rainer Maria Rilke, translated by Robert Lowell and taken from *History* by Robert Lowell, reprinted by permission of Faber and Faber.

p22   'Vitaï Lampada' by Henry Newbolt, reprinted by permission of Peter Newbolt.

p28   'Dirge of Dead Sisters' by Rudyard Kipling, from *Rudyard Kipling's Verse: Definitive Edition*, Hodder & Stoughton, 1940, reprinted by permission of A. P. Watt Ltd on behalf of The National Trust for Places of Historical Interest or Natural Beauty.

p29   'The Hyaenas' by Rudyard Kipling, from *Rudyard Kipling's Verse: Definitive Edition*, Hodder & Stoughton, 1940, reprinted by permission of A. P. Watt Ltd on behalf of The National Trust for Places of Historical Interest or Natural Beauty.

p35   'Prelude: The Troops' by Siegfried Sassoon, copyright Siegfried Sassoon by kind permission of George Sassoon.

p42   'The Volunteer' by Herbert Asquith, reprinted by permission of Michael Asquith.

p45   'For the Fallen' by Laurence Binyon, reprinted by permission of The Society of Authors as the Literary Representative of the Estate of Laurence Binyon.

p45   'Dawn on the Somme' by Robert Nichols, reprinted by permission of Mrs Anne Charlton.

p51   'The Other Side' by Gilbert Frankau, from *The Poetical Works Volume 2*, Chatto and Windus, 1923, reprinted by permission of A. P. Watt Ltd on behalf of Timothy d'Arch Smith.

p51   'A Dead Boche' by Robert Graves, from *Fairies and Fusiliers*, Heinemann, 1917, reprinted by permission of Carcanet Press Limited.

p52   'Manslaughter Morning' by A. E. Tomlinson, from *From Emmanuel to the Somme: The War Writings of A. E. Tomlinson*, Lutterworth Press, 1997, reprinted by permission of The Lutterworth Press.

p53   'Counter-Attack' by Siegfried Sassoon, copyright Siegfried Sassoon by kind permission of George Sassoon.

p53   'On the Wire' by Robert Service, reprinted by permission of Mrs Anne Longepe.

p49   'The Song of the Red-Edged Steel' by Gilbert Frankau, from *The Poetical Works Volume 2*, Chatto and Windus, 1923, reprinted by permission of A. P. Watt Ltd on behalf of Timothy d'Arch Smith.

p56   'Comrades: An Episode' by Robert Nichols, reprinted by permission of Mrs Anne Charlton.

p64   'Winter Warfare' by Edgell Rickword, from *Behind The Eyes*, Carcanet, 1976, reprinted by permission of Carcanet Press Limited.

p68   'Died of Wounds' by Siegfried Sassoon, copyright Siegfried Sassoon by kind permission of George Sassoon.

p69   'The Hero' by Siegfried Sassoon, copyright Siegfried Sassoon by kind permission of George Sassoon.

p70   'The General' by Siegfried Sassoon, copyright Siegfried Sassoon by kind permission of George Sassoon.

p70   'Base Details' by Siegfried Sassoon, copyright Siegfried Sassoon by kind permission of George Sassoon.

p71   'Does it Matter?' by Siegfried Sassoon, copyright Siegfried Sassoon by kind permission of George Sassoon.

p71   'Suicide in the Trenches' by Siegfried Sassoon, copyright Siegfried Sassoon by kind permission of George Sassoon.

p58-80   All poems by Wilfred Owen, from *Wilfred Owen: The Complete Poems and Fragments*, edited by Jon Stallworthy © The Executors of Harold Owen's Estate 1963 and 1983 published by Chatto & Windus. Used by permission of The Random House Group Limited.

p87   'Cannon-Fodder' by Alec Waugh, reprinted by permission of Peter Waugh.

p90   'Dead Man's Dump' by Isaac Rosenberg, reprinted by permission of I. O. Horvitch, the literary executor.

p93   'A Dirge of Victory' by Edward Blunkett Dunsany, reproduced with permission of Curtis Brown Ltd, London on behalf of The Lord Dunsany Will Trust © The Lord Dunsany Will Trust.

p94   'The Armistice' by May Cannan, reprinted by permission of Major James Cannan Slater.

p96   'The Farmer Remembers the Somme' by Vance Palmer, reprinted by permission of Equity Trustees Limited, Melbourne, Australia.

p100   'September 1939' by Vera Brittain, included with the permission of Mark Bostridge and Rebecca Williams, her literary exectuors.

p100   'Days Drawing In' by Edith Joy Scovell, from *Shadows of Chrysanthemums and Other Poems*, Routledge, 1944, reprinted by permission of Taylor and Francis.

p102   'Armed for War' by William Henry Davies, reprinted by permission of K. P. Griffin, Trustee, H. M. Davies Will Trust.

p102   'The Evacuee' by Ronald Stuart Thomas, from *Collected Poems 1945-1990*, J. M. Dent, 1993, reprinted by permission of The Orion Publishing Group.

p104   'Lie in the Dark and Listen' by Noël Coward, from *Collected Verse*, Methuen Publishing Ltd, 1984, copyright © The Estate of Noël Coward.

p105   'Vergissmeinnicht' from *The Complete Poems* by Keith Douglas, reprinted by permission of Faber and Faber.